Russell A. Pitts is a former naval officer, lawyer, high school teacher, college professor, and a Buddhist monk. He is a father and grandfather. This is his first novel which was written mostly on an iPhone. He and his wife, Lori, own and operate a bed and breakfast in Upstate New York.

This fantasy is dedicated to all those who believe that there is a world that exists alongside our everyday world. To those who believe that there is a world of spirits that keep our world in balance.

It is also dedicated to my wife, Lori, whose respect and belief in the power of the natural world inspires me daily.

Russell A. Pitts

The Clonfert House Chronicles Part 1: The Enchanters

Austin Macauley Publishers™
LONDON · CAMBRIDGE · NEW YORK · SHARJAH

Copyright © Russell A. Pitts (2021)

All rights reserved. No part of this publication may be reproduced, distributed, or transmitted in any form or by any means, including photocopying, recording, or other electronic or mechanical methods, without the prior written permission of the publisher, except in the case of brief quotations embodied in critical reviews and certain other noncommercial uses permitted by copyright law. For permission requests, write to the publisher.

Any person who commits any unauthorized act in relation to this publication may be liable to criminal prosecution and civil claims for damages.

This is a work of fiction. Names, characters, businesses, places, events, locales, and incidents are either the products of the author's imagination or used in a fictitious manner. Any resemblance to actual persons, living or dead, or actual events is purely coincidental

Ordering Information
Quantity sales: Special discounts are available on quantity purchases by corporations, associations, and others. For details, contact the publisher at the address below.

Publisher's Cataloging-in-Publication data
Pitts, Russell A.
The Clonfert House Chronicles Part 1: The Enchanters

ISBN 9781647506520 (Paperback)
ISBN 9781647506513 (Hardback)
ISBN 9781647506537 (ePub e-book)

Library of Congress Control Number 2021900439

www.austinmacauley.com/us

First Published (2021)
Austin Macauley Publishers LLC
40 Wall Street, 33rd Floor, Suite 3302
New York, NY 10005
USA

mail-usa@austinmacauley.com
+1 (646) 5125767

I would like to thank Professor Jill Eggers, MFA, of the Art Department of Grand Valley University for her editorial and proofreading help and suggestions.

Prelude

Excerpt From
Liber Secreto De Finbar Mag Aedha
Ship's Scriviner to
the Reverend Captain Brendan
Translated by
Magister Malachi Toibin[1]
Clonfert House, Galway, Ireland

---

[1] TRANSLATOR'S NOTE: there are two records of this voyage by Saint Brendan: the one excerpted here and the public record which details a fictitious voyage. The latter was a faint to distract anyone then, or in future, from discovering the truth of the voyage. The *Liber Secreto* was discovered in 1969, hidden beneath a stack of charts of moon phases associated with the bays and harbors of 'The Land of the Saints,' the final destination of the voyage detailed in the *Liber Secreto*. The precise location of 'The Land of the Saints' has never been determined, although scholars suspect it was either Labrador or Prince Edward Island, Canada. This volume has been subject to a campaign of discredit by those forces in the world who know the danger to them that is contained in the *Liber Secreto*. They have made and will continue to make every attempt to secure the *Liber Secreto* and place it in the Vatican archives where it would no doubt disappear. Fortunately, Clonfert House has been equally aggressive in protecting the *Liber Secreto*. The danger the *Liber Secreto* contains is irrefutable truth of Saint Brendan's landing in North America almost a thousand years before Columbus. For the Vatican, or any other authority to recognize the *Liber Secreto* as true, would undermine much of western history and tradition.

We had just weathered a ferocious gale and our main mast was splintered. The Reverend Captain Brendan, who was also the ship's navigator, had set the sail makers to freeing the mast from the twisted sheets of the sails. He ordered the timber smiths to ignite the forge so as to fashion braces for the fractured mast. Here, below deck with me, the ship's physician busied himself preparing various tonics to quell the sloshing stomachs of the deckhands who were doing their best to repair the damage on the deck above us. For my part, I stayed well back in the shadows of my quarters in the stern of the ship, all the better to protect that which was entrusted to me. I sensed threats beyond the shadows.

"Land ho," a voice cried out from the bow. All hands went silent. A lone gull cried in the distance, a sure sign of land.

Reverend Captain Brendan's voice shattered the silence. "Busy yourselves, men! If we can't make our way ashore soon enough, we surely will be repelled by the tide and will be adrift. Turn to!"

As he spoke, I crept up through a hatch in a nearby hold to listen. As soon as his last words rang out, all hands returned to their tasks with a fevered determination. I slipped back into the shadows below deck. As the ship's scrivener, I was charged with recording the events of our voyage. At least that was what everyone believed. And well, they should have, for I made a show each sunset of presenting myself at Reverend Captain Brendan's door on the main deck. He had the quartermaster bring out a table so that all could witness the recording of my daily entries in the ship's log. No one knew the other charge I had been commissioned to fulfill by Reverend Captain Brendan.

I held in my quarters in the stern of the ship a cargo that, should anyone know of its existence, would have surely raised a mutiny. Where there is mutiny, there is death. My own possible death was a price, Reverend Captain Brendan informed me, I must be willing to pay. When I became familiar with this precious cargo, I pledged my life without pause or reservation. Reverend Captain Brendan and I had sailed many times before and we enjoyed a deep, mutual trust. I must confess, however, that my keeping of this, my secret log, he would see as a violation of that trust. But, for reasons that are not yet clear to me, I have no choice but to record this secret history of our journey.

I lived each day in fear of discovery, not just of this volume but of the cargo I was guarding. I knew and trusted only five men aboard that vessel: Reverend Captain, the First Mate, Purser, Quartermaster, and Physician. I remained completely ignorant and fearful of the rest of the rough, coarse seamen who inhabited that ship. Most, to my dismay, were of foreign complexion and tongue.

On the eve of that voyage, Reverend Captain Brendan assembled the five of us at the seamen's chapel adjacent to the dock where our ship laid at moor. It was then, under cover of the darkness and fog, that Reverend Captain Brendan shared with us the nature of our voyage.

As a missionary priest of the Roman Church, Reverend Captain Brendan had been dispatched to the British Isles to convert all who lived there to Catholicism. Reverend Captain Brendan had garnered a well-deserved reputation for his many successes.

"However," he said, "this voyage we are about to undertake is not part of my missionary work, though it must take on the appearance of it. Should the church discover our purpose, we all be ex-communicated, if not put to death, and thereafter be confined in the depths of hell for all eternity. At least that is what the church would have us believe. Our voyage, as I will soon explain, has a simple end. We will remove from these green hills and valleys proof that there is life beneath the soil. That beneath the hillocks, mounds, and trees there is a world of creatures that protect and preserve the way of the wind and the woods. If the church should ever be able to find them, I fear they will eradicate these creatures. Should that happen, then the world will lose all sense of balance. I am filled with dread at this prospect and believe, beyond any doubt, that our task is to remove these creatures to shelter near safer waters."

I knew Reverend Captain Brendan to be a man of deep faith. It seemed peculiar to me that he would even mention the existence of the fairy folk. His church saw them as either folktales or the work of the devil. But I had trust in Reverend Captain Brendan. If he was willing to undertake this mission, then I would surely be his colleague.

We sat silently as he let his words hang in the air. We all looked at one another, perhaps wondering who among us shared Reverend Captain Brendan's beliefs. I did, for reasons that I will explain later, should there be time and opportunity to do so. As we looked for some signs in one another, we knew, without exchanging a word, that each of us held fast to the same beliefs.

The activity on the deck above requited. I heard the sails unfurl. The tide was running high. The boatswain ordered all hands to their posts. The ship shuttered to port. The waves escorted us closer to the shore. The landing boats were boarded with the exploring crew. I waited here below the deck for Reverend Captain's orders. They came shortly after the anchor dropped.

I now find myself about to set foot on this unknown shore. I had not been given any further instructions on what to do when this moment arrived. I must have faith in Reverend Captain Brendan. All I had been told was, "We have arrived at 'The Land of the Saints.'"

Chapter One

Enniskellin, Ireland
Saint Brendan's Academy
Master Chan Wu's
Dinner Party—Arriving

"I hope you boys realize what an honor this is to be invited to Master Chan Wu's house for dinner." Kevin O'Connell's father was more excited than Kevin and his classmate Michael Tynan were, and they were really excited! Kevin and Michael looked at each other and wondered why his father was absolutely giddy with excitement, even though all he was doing was dropping them off at Master Chan Wu's house.

"When I was a student at Saint Brendan's, I'd heard rumors about these dinners, but not once during my eight years as a student did I know anyone who had actually been to one. Do you boys know anyone who has been to Master Chan Wu's house?" He looked back at the two boys in the rearview mirror searching for some sign that, yes, they knew someone who had.

"I don't, Mister O'Connell," Michael said.

"Kevin?" he asked.

"Sorry, Dad, no. I don't know anyone who's been there. We have heard the rumors though."

Mr. O'Connell sighed, adjusted the mirror back into place, and got lost in his thoughts.

Kevin and Michael, both sixteen years old, were in their sixth year of the eight-year program at Saint Brendan's Academy in Enniskellin. They started hearing the rumors of Master Chan Wu's dinner parties shortly after mid-term exams of their first year. The rumors ranged from being inducted into some secret Chinese cult to being informed that while you could remain at the academy through the end of the eight years, you would not be of sufficient character or achievement to advance to one of the Saint Brendan Universities. You would be sent to one of the public universities, maybe even Trinity in Dublin, all expenses paid. Once your degree was completed, you would be employed by Clonfert House in some capacity that insured that your enchanting skills were never used again. In some cases, it was rumored that you simply disappeared. Kevin and Michael were sure that the news that was coming their way was that they were going to become 'publics.' This was Kevin's father's fate.

There seemed to be some substance to the rumors about Master Chan Wu's dinner parties. Michael recalled the year that Jorge Macado went missing after attending one of Master Chan Wu's dinners. Speaking on behalf of Jorge's parents, Master Chan Wu assured the headmaster that Jorge was fine, but would not be returning. Apparently, the headmaster didn't challenge Master Chan Wu. Jorge never returned anyone's phone calls, failed to send a single text, having no emails, no Instagram, and his Facebook page seemed frozen in time. There was not a single update on his timeline until a year later when a picture of a mountain hut deeply covered in snow appeared. Not a picture of Jorge, just the hut. Then, nothing more. When Master Chan Wu was asked about Jorge during one of his classes, all he was supposed to have said was, "Picking tea is harder than drinking tea." No one had any idea what he meant.

Another piece of evidence about some student's fate was presented to the students at the end of each year when there were always a few graduating students whose names were never mentioned at the final convocation. Their rooms were empty of any trace of them. Protocol forbade asking about them. It was as if they had never been students at all. No one ever heard from them again.

Michael didn't know if Kevin was thinking about these rumors as they turned the corner onto the wide boulevard where Master Chan Wu lived, but Michael was certain that they were going to be informed that their final years at Saint Brendan's Academy would not, absolutely could not, under any circumstances lead to admission in one of the universities. Both Kevin and Michael would be a disgrace to their families.

Over six hundred years ago, both Kevin's family and Michael's had been part of the thirteen founding families of Saint Brendan's. Every boy and girl in each of the families had not only attended Saint Brendan's here, or at one of the other seven locations around the world, but each had also gone on to great success as Enchanters. Not a single descendent of the founding families had failed to become an Enchanter, except for Kevin's father who was able to return a normal life, which was unusual. Kevin didn't know what happened or why, and he never asked. Michael was convinced that Kevin and he were about to learn to share the same fate.

Michael's maternal ancestor, Moira McSweeney, a legendary Enchantress, was the one who tamed the Cu Fail, a once-fierce hound that today is known as the Irish Wolf Hound. Kevin had an ancestor, Seamus O'Connell, who is famous for having brokered a peace between the Tuatha De Danaan and their arch enemies, the Fomorie, that still stands to this day. Kevin's uncle, Finnean O'Connell, is currently the Regent of Clonfert House where those personally selected by the Council of Elders study for their doctorates in Neuro-Enchantment and Transcendental Movement. Michael's Aunt Sheila is a special advisor to the Council of Elders on the uses of Aos Si Enchantments. Needless to say, their poor showing, as was about to be explained to them by Master Chan Wu, would be a black mark in the annals of both their houses.

"Michael, why do you think the master has invited us? Do you think we are about to become members of some secret Chinese cult? Learn Kung Fu? Become Shaolin fighting monks?" Kevin was antsy. He couldn't sit still. Kevin had a reputation for being dramatic and he was proud of it. On more than one occasion, he was known to provide fantastical embellishments for anyone who would listen. It was one of the many things that bound him and Michael together as fast friends.

"Don't know, Kevin. Maybe we aren't doing very well and he's about to tell us we can never get our degrees as Enchanters," Michael said.

Kevin sat absolutely still. He looked at the back of his father's head, searching for some reaction. Mister O'Connell was still lost in whatever imaginings he was having.

"Shut up, Michael!" he whispered. "If my father hears you, I'll be in for it even before we know why we're here. I don't want to fail like he did."

"What's that, Kevin? Did you say something?" Mister O'Connell asked via the rearview mirror.

"Not to you, Dad. Michael and I were just talking about school. Just stuff, you know." Kevin shot Michael a don't-say-anything-else look.

"What's the address again, Michael?" Mister O'Connell asked me.

"2558. The house there is 2418, so we are getting close," Michael said as he leaned up close behind Mr. O'Connell to make sure he heard him. Mister O'Connell was known for asking questions and paying absolutely no attention to the answer and then asking the question again—at least three more times.

"Got it. 2558."

Even Mister O'Connell was acting differently tonight.

Master Chan Wu's house sat on a broad landscaped boulevard just on the eastern end of town. When Kevin and Michael had asked around about it, no one seemed to know specifically where he lived. Again, rumors abounded about the master and his house. There were some students who were convinced he didn't live in a house at all. They believed he lived in a different dimension when he wasn't in class or his office. What a mystery he fostered about his personal life!

"Here it is, 2558." Mister O'Connell announced 'here it is' in a booming voice, but was breathless when he said '2558.' When the two boys looked out the window, they understood why.

The master's house was nothing like the other houses on the boulevard. The other houses were mini-mansions that looked like they were trying to be French chateaux or Italian palazzos. Not one of them succeeded. The master's house couldn't really be seen, at least not most of it. What the boys noticed first was the glow.

The house was surrounded by a high brick wall that was topped with clay tiles that made the wall look like it had a miniature peaked roof running its entire length. Above the wall, they could just make out the roof peak of what must be his house. It was slightly hidden inside mature bamboo, but its peak soared into the night sky. Everything was bathed in a warm crimson glow. Everything about this place, the wall, the bamboo, the peak of the house visible above it all, reminded Michael of Chinese temples he had seen in National Geographic documentaries. The only entrance through the wall was an enormous wooden gate that was flanked by two equally enormous Foo Dog statues. The whole thing gave the impression of a model of a hidden Chinese city.

"Wow!" Michael said under his breath.

Kevin just stared, equally amazed at the sight.

"This is something," was all Mister O'Connell could say.

"Just drop us by the gate, Dad. We'll take it from there." Kevin didn't want his father to get any ideas about trying to come inside with them just to take a peak.

"Are you sure? I'll bet I can drive through once the gate opens."

"Yes, Dad, I'm sure. I'll call when we're ready to get picked up," Kevin said anxiously.

"Alright. Maybe I can drive in to pick you up," Mister O'Connell said, holding out hope.

Michael didn't say anything and motioned for Kevin to get out of the car.

Mister O'Connell drove off while Kevin and Michael approached the gate without saying a word to each other.

"I don't see a handle or bell. Do you?" Kevin asked as he ran his hands over the surface of the wooden gate. Michael joined him searching the worn surface, but couldn't find anything that indicated there was a way to open it. Then, to their surprise, the gate started to swing open. They stood there as the gate slowly swung back to reveal a flagstone path that led through the thick bamboo to stairs leading up to the house.

The courtyard! It was a courtyard because this was something altogether different from a front yard of an ordinary house. It was hung with Chinese lanterns that were the source of the red glow the two boys had seen from the street. There was a flagstone path leading to steps that rose up to the front door of the house. The entire house seemed to be floating in the air. The steps, Michael counted twenty-seven of them, ran completely around the house, giving the house a look as though it hovered above the earth. The house seemed to be just a single story, though a very large single-story house. From where they stood, it was not possible to get a true appreciation of its scale. Or, Michael thought, maybe it was just another one of the master's illusions. The interior of the house shimmered with a golden light that shone through the paper screens that made up all the exterior walls. Shoji screens, Michael thought, they were called. The only indication of a front entrance was a set of handrails leading up the center of stairs in front of them. Just as they started up the steps, the screen at the top of the stairs slid open.

"Ah, Mister Tynan and Mister O'Connell, right on time as requested. Please, remove your shoes and come inside." Master Chan Whu was dressed more casually than they had ever seen him. He wore simple black pants, black silk mandarin jacket embroidered with a golden dragon, and snow-white socks. They removed their shoes and stepped through the screen into a vast room.

Michael was right about the Shoji screens. They made up the exterior walls. Master Chan Wu had arranged the room they entered so that the furniture created various-sized conversation areas. There must have been at least nine different areas. Each one seemed to have a theme of some sort because the chairs, sofas, tables, lamps, and books in each were coordinated. Yet, each area was somehow different. The boys couldn't figure how, but they knew they were. Spreading across the entire expanse of the room was a gigantic oriental carpet.

"Please, come this way and have a seat, here," the master said, indicating they should sit on a sofa in one of the smallest areas on the fringe of the room. They assumed the master would sit in the chair opposite them. "I'll be right back," the master said before he disappeared.

"Can you believe this place?" Kevin said, wide-eyed.

"Pretty amazing," was all Michael could say. Kevin and Michael surveyed the room. They noticed that there were some interior walls at the opposite end from where they were sitting. That must be where the rest of the house was. They couldn't tell where the master had gone.

"First, some tea." The master materialized in front of them, setting down a tray on the coffee table between them. Neither one of them saw him come back.

Master Chan Wu poured the tea into small cups without saying a word. When the three cups were filled, he handed one to Kevin and one to Michael. He looked at the two boys slowly with his dark eyes and then raised his cup slightly in the air. They mimicked him, not knowing what else to do.

"May the spirits guide us!" he said. The boys drank their tea in one gulp. Master Chan Wu reached out and took their cups.

"Now for dinner! I have much to tell you and even more to ask of you," the master said as he stood up, indicating they should follow him.

Chapter Two

Enniskellin, Ireland
Saint Brendan's Academy
Master Chan Wu's Dinner Party—Dinner

Kevin followed Master Chan Wu a little too enthusiastically, prompting the master to turn and admonish him with an intense look. He and Michael continued on towards a set of large sliding screens with two red-necked cranes painted on them. A barely visible light glowed through the opaque screens, giving the impression that the cranes were in flight. Neither of the boys had noticed them when they first came into the house, but there was much about this house that seemed hidden just beyond their sight. Just as they drew close enough for the master to reach out to slide the screens open, a shadow appeared on the screen, parting them to reveal a massive room.

Kevin turned to Michael, wide-eyed and awestruck. Michael was as well. The room was so large that they could not make out the far wall. Seeing the house from the outside revealed nothing of its depths. Kevin and Michael followed the master into the room. The screens slid closed behind them. It was then the shadow they had seen behind the screen revealed herself.

"Gentlemen, this is my daughter, Ai Su Wu," the master said over his shoulder as he continued to lead them towards the table.

"It is my pleasure to finally meet you two young men," she said as she breezed past them to step beside her father.

"What has the master said about us?" Kevin whispered to Michael.

"Who knows? I'm sure we will find out soon enough," Michael answered. The truth was that Michael didn't like the fact that she knew who they were. He couldn't tell if she was serious about meeting them or being ironic. Both of the boys were starting to feel uneasy.

Kevin tried to break the mood. "Look at the size of this place." Kevin was looking up towards the ceiling.

Above them, the heavy beams and rafters soared to the peak of the roof. It must have been at least thirty feet high. Each beam and rafter was lacquered in black. They shimmered in the amber glow from the lanterns that hung from the beams. The room was dominated by a colossal wooden table. It was lacquered in a blood-red color. Around the perimeter of the tabletop were inlaid golden dragons similar to the ones of Master Chan Wu's jacket. It took Michael a minute to realize that each of the dragons was separated by some sort of glyph or rune. He didn't recognize them. Neither did Kevin.

"Oh no," Kevin said under his breath. "I can't believe they are here." He raised his left hand slightly to point to the table.

Sitting to the left of the seat at the head of the table were the fifteen-year-old Temne twins, Minda and Affey. They were variously known at school as the 'oddities,' or sometimes the 'harpies,' depending on how they treated you. They were descendants of those original signers of the Clonfert Compact, just as Kevin and Michael were. Their ancestors were from the African continent. They were of royal blood from the Dyula and Kissi peoples. When their ancestors fled the slave traffickers in the eighteenth century, they made their way to Georgia in the United States, where they became known as the Gula-Gheechee people, often *Gulah* for short. The Temne twins spoke several languages, including the languages that were on the verge of extinction in their ancestry.

Minda Temne was spirited, confident, and aggressive. Affey was different. Affey was quiet and shy. Where Minda wasted no take in staking out a position or expressing an opinion, Affey was reticent to say much of anything. Kevin was convinced Minda really was a harpy, given the disdain with which she seemed to throw in his direction. Kevin thought Affey was nice, but under her sister's thumb. Michael had had few encounters with them. They were a year behind the boys, but a year ahead of Michael and Kevin in many of their classes. Rumor had it that they possessed some sort of prodigious skill. Kevin and Michael really didn't care about that. They just wanted to stay clear of them. Now here they were, cornered in Master Chan Wu's house with them. If Kevin and Michael were about to be dismissed, then were the Temne Twins here to be the witnesses?

"I know the four of you are acquainted," Master Chan Wu said with a glint in his eye. "Mister O'Connell, you sit there." The master indicated that Kevin should sit opposite Affey. "Mister Tynan, there," he said, pointing Michael to the seat across from Minda.

"Hi, Kevin," Minda said with a broad smile.

"Hello." That was the best Kevin could do under the circumstances.

"Now, before we have our first course," began the master.

His daughter appeared behind him. How she appeared, none of the four could say. She just appeared. "There is a call for you," she said, handing Master Chan Wu a cellphone.

"Who is it?"

"They didn't say, Father." Her tone was respectful but firm. She made it clear that he should take the call.

"Please, excuse me while I deal with this annoyance." Master Chan Wu left the table, disappearing into the shadows of the room.

His daughter said, "I will be back in a few minutes with the first course. If my father has not yet returned, then please begin. I will join you shortly." Like her father, she evaporated in the shadows.

Minda broke the silence, sitting right in the middle of the table between them. "Oh, Kevin, my sister is so excited that you are here, aren't you, Affey?" She put her arm around her twin sister who just kept staring down at the table. "Come on, Affey, you've been waiting a long time to talk to Kevin." Minda fixed her gaze on Kevin. Kevin tried glaring back, but backed down and stared at the table, a mirror image of Affey. Minda shifted her attention to Michael.

"And you, Michael Tynan, you are not so much a surprise to me as a disappointment. Obviously, Master Chan Wu sees something special in you. I can't imagine what that might be." She removed her arm from around her sister. She leaned forward, propping her elbows on the table and then framing her face in her hands. She fixed her eyes on Michael. He stared right back at her. "Michael, Michael," she sighed. "What secrets have you been keeping from us? I would have thought that anyone with some unusual gift would have demonstrated it by now. Or, Michael, maybe you're just a fraud."

Kevin had heard enough. "Shut up, Minda. If you only knew..." He froze mid-sentence. Michael knew exactly what Minda was doing.

"You know that we are not allowed to use enchantments on each other. It's a rule. Why are you bending his thoughts?" Using enchantments on each other was strictly forbidden, except in highly unusual circumstances which, the dean of Saint Brendan's insisted, never occurred.

"You are such a stick in the mud, Michael. Rules are made to be broken." She dropped her face from her hands to fiddle with her napkin.

"What was I saying?" Minda had released Kevin.

"You were about to say something about the dragons on the table. I think," Affey intervened on Kevin's behalf. She looked at him apologetically. Michael was beginning to get the gist of Minda's first comments. Affey must have a thing for Kevin. Just then, Master Chan Wu returned.

"My apologies. It is rather rude to leave one's guests. You must all remember that." He looked at each one of them in turn as if he was burning his advice onto their brains. "Our first course tonight is a soup my ancestors first made over two thousand years ago. It will clear your palate so that the delicacies you will be served tonight can be fully appreciated."

His daughter, Ai Su Wu, returned to the table followed by three small men of vague ancestry. They were tiny. Yet, they appeared ancient in some way. They were very handsome. They were dressed identically to Master Chan Wu, but without the embroidered dragon. Course after course was served by these three men. Conversation over the course of the meal was uneventful, except for when Kevin strongly objected to one dish that smelled terrible but looked appealing. It wasn't. Master Chan Wu and his daughter got a hardy laugh as he choked this course down. The rest of the dishes were some of the best foods the students had ever eaten, although they had no idea what most of them were.

At one point, Ai Su Wu told the story of a former student of hers. (She revealed that she was a special tutor in Mis-Remembrance and Thought Erasure at Saint Brendan's. She swore the students to secrecy about this.) Her former student, whom she did not name, had been sent to the Fujian Prefecture in China to retrieve a jade broch that held highly a volatile power. While the student was able to get the broch, he disappeared as soon as he arrived in Goa where he was to deliver it to one of Master Chan Wu's colleagues. Neither the student nor the broch had been found. The students didn't know why she told them this story. It had one positive effect—Minda remained silent for the rest of dinner.

The three tiny men cleared the table. Ai Su Wu excused herself. Once they had left the room, Master Chan Wu's mood shifted. During dinner, he was lively, full of amusing anecdotes about other teachers, and really enjoying himself. Now his mood turned serious.

"The fact that the four of you are here is no accident or coincidence. You four have been chosen for a rather serious endeavor. In fact, it is so serious that the future of all of us teachers, students, and the magisterium itself depends on your success. Not now, Miss Temne," Master Chan Wu said to Minda who was about to ask a question. He continued, "You might want to know why we are asking students, especially students who are as young as you, to undertake this task instead of someone like myself or someone from Clonfert House. The truth is that only you four hold among you the combination of the enchanting kills and powers necessary for what we need. Believe me when I say we tried every combination of students across the entire magisterium. Only the four of you met the criteria for this most serious matter."

"What if we refuse?" Minda said, with just a hint of defiance in her voice.

Master Chan Wun turned slowly to face her. He leaned in very close to her. She didn't retreat, even an inch.

"Refuse, Miss Temne, and I will personally erase not just your memory of Saint Brendan's, but I will also eradicate every last trace of enchantment in you."

No one had a clue what Minda thought at that moment, but the other three were terrified. Was this their only option?

Michael looked at Minda. He wished he could tell her that he was on her side and would do whatever she asked if they could get out of whatever Master Chan Wu had in store for them. Kevin's legs were trembling so hard that the table started to shake.

"Calm down, Mister O'Connell," Master Chan Wu said as he placed his hand firmly on Kevin's shoulder. "We will not send you off without preparation. Everything will be successful if you abide by what we instruct you to do." The master then addressed all of them, "I will be your guide through this. I will not abandon you, although I may not be physically present with you."

Ai Su Wu reappeared at the table with four identical blue folders. Each was wrapped in a single silver ribbon that was fastened together with a wax seal of the magisterium. She handed one to each of the four students.

She told them, "You must now read what is in this folder. My father and I will leave you for a while so that you can read this very carefully. When you have finished, we will return. We will answer any questions you have." With that being said, she and Master Chan Wu vanished from the room. The master did not say a word. The four students looked at one another. Minda tried to put on airs that she wasn't really interested in reading what was in the folder. Affey's hands shook and she kept looking at Kevin for reassurance. Kevin looked at Affey for help. As for Michael, he was afraid of what was in the folder, but couldn't wait to read it. The four of them shared one last look and then opened our folders. This is what was inside:

THE FINAL TESTAMENT OF
FINBAR MAG AEDHA
TRANSLATED BY
MAGISTER MALACHI TOIBIN
CLONFERT HOUSE, GALWAY, IRELAND

One hundred and twenty-seven days have passed since Reverend Captain Brendan brought us here to these dismal shores. I have tried with utmost diligence to maintain my secret journal, but alas! Events have overtaken me. My once-secret journal has vanished, along with every trace of my charges. As I set ink to parchment today, dread and misery have spread over me. I fear my time on this Earth is fast approaching its conclusion. I am compelled to record this, my final testament, even though I have grave doubt it, or I, will never be found. Should some mercy spare me, then this testament will not have been necessary. Yet, I feel abandoned here by heaven, so I shall leave this testament in hope that it will be found along with the treasure I have lost. I shall now record as best I can what has transpired in the past several days that has led to my pending demise.

Reverend Captain Brendan departed with a partial crew on the night of a full moon with a king tide. He did not want to raise any suspicions, should his absence from the Gaelic shores be discovered. His final words to me were, "You must protect these creatures even unto your own death. Should you fail, the wisdom of the world, yea, the Wisdom of God Himself, will fall into the wrong hands. You, Master Mag Aedha, are the only guardian these wee folks have in these unknown parts. Be vigilant. No matter what may befall you, they must establish a firm foothold here so that the balance between the opposing forces in the world is maintained." He did not await my response. I stood on the shore, powerless to stop him. As the sails of his ship slipped beneath the horizon, I wept.

Much has transpired since his departure. My only solace during the past days has been a dark fellow who worked the crow's nest on the boat, who calls himself Daryush Jal. He shared with me his belief in the 'spenta mainyu' of his Muslim faith. He has given me sworn assurances that these 'spenta mainyu' are good, kind, spirits and perhaps relatives of my charges. For him, the 'spenta mainyu' and the spirits in my charge were sent by God to maintain order, justice, compassion, and happiness. When I awoke several days ago to discover the fairies and my secret journal had disappeared, I sought Daryush Jal's advice.

The first thing he did was retreat into the forest that surrounded us to 'abide in the present circumstances,' as he put it. I implored him to let me accompany him, but he refused. As the sun was lowering in the west, he returned. "They are gone, Master Mag Aedha. They will not return. I fear, however, that they did not depart on their own, but were enticed away by false pretenses. They are in grave circumstances. There is nothing we can do. They have been removed to a place beyond our capacity to enter. I have prayed to my ancestors to implore the 'spenta mainyu' to intervene. We must be patient and await some sign."

"But surely, we..." He held up his hand to silence me.

"These matters are not for us mortals to resolve. We have neither the power nor the influence to change the course that lie ahead for them. Only others, such as the

'spenta mainyu,' have any chance of rescuing them." He *spoke so calmly and assuredly that he eased my deepening terror for at least a while.*

"So, what shall we do?" I asked.

"Prepare to depart ourselves. We must also inform the rest of the men of these events."

Despite my reluctance to do so, I called the remaining members of the crew into assembly and shared with them only that the spirits had departed. The rest I kept between Daryush Jal and myself.

One of their numbers, who had emerged as their leader, stepped forward menacingly. The men left behind by Reverend Captain Brendan were all heathens who had abandoned God. To them, our voyage with the wee folk was cursed. Now, so were we all. The only hope they expressed was that as the days passed, the fairy folk would meet with misfortune, thus sparing them from the torture the fairies were planning for all of us. Would that they had kept their hope to themselves!

Their leader began, "This is your fault, Master Mag Aedha. The captain was clear in his charge to you. You have failed miserably. You and that dark fellow there can do as you wish, but my men and I are leaving." The men stood behind him defiantly.

"There is nowhere for you to go. We are surrounded by these dense, dark woods. You have no boats to set out on the sea." I attempted to persuade them that they had no option but to remain here. I also feared that their departure would expose Daryush Jal and I to whatever menace had descended on the fairies and taken them away.

"We shall take our chances through the woods," he spat his words at me. *"We will leave you enough provisions and supplies to last a few weeks. In that time, if we will have secured rescue, then we will return to fetch you. If not, then we'll have probably perished, as will you."* The men then made their way to their quarters as the sky grew dark.

"Leave them to depart," was all that Daryush Jal said. Before he went to his hut, he turned to me and said, *"Tomorrow, we begin anew. Do not despair or we will be doomed."* I was left alone.

I slept restlessly that night, plagued by dreams of boiling seas where monsters rose up from the depths to devour everything in their path. The bones of men and splinters from the hulls of ships floated on the waves. Screams of agony pierced the air while a distant song called me to its source. I awoke before sunrise, shaking with fright. My dream, I was certain, was a portent of what was yet to come. As I lay there trembling, Daryush Jal came crashing through the curtain that served as my door.

"Master Mag Aedha. Come quickly, the 'spenta mainyu' have heard our prayers. They have left us a gift of tremendous value. Come, come. You must see." He grabbed me by the arm and hoisted me up out of my misery. His strength belied his small stature. He pulled me furiously toward the edge of the forest. The sun was just rising over the sea behind us, casting a soft light into the trees. Suddenly, he stopped. I crashed into his back.

"There, near that large oak. Do you see it?" His voice was hushed and reverent.

I saw it. A ray of sunshine struck the golden lid on what, from where we stood, looked like a sea captain's chest. As the sun rose higher, sun ray after sun ray illuminated the chest. We looked at each other and then ran to inspect it.

Just as I was about to lay my hands on what appeared to be the lock, Daryush Jal stopped me.

"We must first say a prayer of gratitude." He closed his eyes and lowered his head. I did the same. He uttered not a word, nor did I, but something inside me was profoundly thankful. We stood this way for several minutes before he spoke.

"Now, master, before we open it, let us make sure we examine the exterior first. Perhaps there is something on the outside we must know first."

He worked his way around one side while I made my way around the other. The chest was covered in runes. I knew they were runes from my earlier experiences with Reverend Captain Brendan. Yet, I did not recognize them. What they said, the meanings they held, or warnings they issued were not revealed. Daryush Jal scratched his beard. Clearly, he had no more insight into the runes than I did. We next turned our attention to the lock.

It was a large, bronze lock with a single keyhole. It was a common-enough lock with no etchings or other marks to indicate there was anything unusual about it. Daryush Jal tugged at the mechanism to see if it was freed. It was securely engaged. There was no key left for us to use.

"We should move this into my lodgings," I said. Daryush Jal nodded his agreement.

When we reached down underneath the chest to lift it up, we were astonished to discover that it was extraordinarily lightweight, given its size and golden properties. We carried it to my lodgings and set it against the back wall, as far from the door as possible.

"What shall we do now?" I asked aloud to no one in particular.

"We shall know when we shall know," was all that Daryush Jal offered. He then took up a position on the floor opposite the chest where he sat with eyes closed for the rest of the day. Something was surely required of us, I thought.

We hadn't eaten, so I left to soak some salted fish in a pail of the rainwater we collected. While they moistened, I went into the woods for some of the eatable greens that carpeted the forest floor. It was during this foray into the forest that the most extraordinarily disturbing event took place.

I was deep enough in the woods to be hidden from Daryush Jal, but not so deep that I could not see my lodging. I had just picked the last leaf I needed and was standing up to return to the clearing that was our home when a creature appeared on a branch of the tree that hung just above my head. This was an unfamiliar creature. It bore no resemblance whatsoever to any of the fairies once under my charge. Whether it was male or female, I could not say. It was dressed too elegantly for a woodsy spirit. Its clothes were not of a fashion I had ever seen. It looked down on me with large greenish eyes. Never in my life had I ever been so mesmerized by another being. Then it spoke. Not words, but in thoughts.

'The chest will open in two days hence. You must be patient as you are being observed. Tamper with the chest in the slightest way and it will vanish just as your fairies and journal have vanished. Should you pass this test, then the *chest will open. What you will discover therein are the secrets of the fairies, the 'spenta mainyu,' and all of the invisible spirits that keep your world in equilibrium. Those secrets will be entrusted to you and your descendants. Fail at this test as you failed in protecting the spirits and you will be responsible for the chaos that shall engulf you all. Two days more, Master Mag Aedha, two days more is all that is required.'*

I was about to inquire of him as to why all this had happened when he turned to mist and was carried away on a breeze.

When I told Daryush Jal what had happened, he just smiled and said, "Two days. Not much to ask of us, is it?"

For the next two days, we enjoyed pleasant weather. We caught the most tender of fish in the lagoon. Daryush Jal, during one of his extended sojourns into the woods, had come upon a fruit tree which bore large yellow-colored fruit. The fruit was sweet and plump with juice. There was no need for patience during these two days. It was as if nature had conspired to ease us through them.

Daryush Jal and I spent the second night together lying on our mats in front of the chest, anticipating the dawn when the chest was to open. When the dawn broke, Daryush Jal and I awoke to foul weather. The sea was agitated. Moody clouds were rising in the east. The wind was growing increasingly fierce. I was alarmed. When I looked at Darush Jal to take the measure of him, I saw that he too was in a panic.

"Daryush, what shall we do? What does this mean?" I was on the verge of tears.

"I don't know, Master Mag Aedha. I am certain that this has to do with the chest."

A bolt of lightning struck a nearby tree, splitting it in two. We both closed our eyes, fearing this was our demise. I reached out to grab Daryush Jal for consolation, but before I could embrace him, everything stopped. The wind ceased howling, the sea became silent, and everything was still. We turned to face the chest.

The lock clicked and slowly pivoted so that it could now be removed. We both hesitated, uncertain of whether to remove it or not. I took it upon myself to move closer to remove the lock from the latch. I was no more than an inch or two from touching it when it fell away on its own accord. The lid creaked open. By now, Daryush Jal had crept up next to me and we were kneeling in front of the chest. Together, we peered over the edge.

Inside the golden chest were scrolls, far too many of them to count without removing them all from the chest. Without so much as a whisper, Daryush Jal reached in and withdrew one of the scrolls. It was bound with a blue leather filament. There was a tag attached to the string on which was written several of the unknown runes. Next, I reached in and withdrew another scroll. This one was tied with a magenta thread, to which was affixed a similar tag, but with different runes. For the next several hours, we removed all of the scrolls so that we had an inventory of how many there were. In all, there were one hundred and eight scrolls. We did not unroll any of them, choosing to leave them intact for later study. Once we had counted the scrolls, we returned them to the chest. As soon as the last scroll was set in place, the weather grew nasty again. The chest slammed shut. The lock flew into place and closed. Once more, the lightning struck nearby. Rain fell in hard pellets. We attempted to keep the weather at bay from my door, but to no avail. The wind, the rain, and nature itself infiltrated my lodgings.

"Master Mag Aedha? Master Mag Aedha?" the question was carried hauntingly on the wind.

"There you are, Master Mag Aedha." Standing in the threshold of my hut was a creature of medium stature. Even though the wind and rain swirled around her, she remained unaffected by it. Her hair was raven-black, as were her eyes. His crimson robes billowed gracefully despite the gale force winds. "And you, Daryush Jal. I wasn't sure you would remain here. After all, you do not enjoy much of a reputation for loyalty or steadfastness. This truly is most auspicious." She floated over to the chest.

"Who are you, mistress?" Daryush Jal asked.

"It matters not who I am. What matters, Master Jal, is that I know you and I know this scrivener. His journal is most intriguing." She turned to face me; her eyes ablaze.

"Before either of you utter another sound, you must be informed that we have come to retrieve what is rightfully ours. That little imp you met two days ago, Master Mag Aedha, was most cooperative when we captured him. My legions are arriving as I speak. Both of you shall be removed to the deepest part of the forest. Thence, your survival is no concern of ours."

I fell into a pitch-black darkness.

All I could recall after hearing her words was awakening near an azure pool somewhere in the forest. I was alone. There was no sign of Daryush Jal. I didn't know how long I remained there by that pond. Eventually, a tribe *of men, scantily clad in leather, hair in long braids, and carrying primitive tools found me. They stripped me bare. They disappeared into the woods. I didn't know if they had left me here to die or stripped my clothes so that I would not flee. I was sure they had left me to be eaten by whatever creatures prowled there in the darkness. I hurriedly wrote this testament with the instruments they left behind. I was confused by this gesture. It almost felt as if they wanted me to record this, my final testament. No matter the reason, I would leave it in a crevice in the rocks I saw above the pond. Whether I survived or not was no longer important to me. I would no doubt succumb to the elements in this forsaken place. I would die in profound remorse for my triple failures. I failed to protect the fairies, I lost my journal, but most importantly, I could not shelter the chest with its scrolls from the harm the raven-haired lady was intent on inflicting on the world.*

May God forgive me!
Signed
Finbar Mag Aedha, Scrivener and Loyal Servant of Reverend Captain Brendan

Affey finished first. She gently closed the folder and slid it away from her. She turned to her sister and said, "I cannot do this, whatever it is. You shouldn't either."

"You heard what Master Chan Wu said. If we don't do what they want, then what do you think will become of us?" Minda spoke to Affey firmly but with concern.

"She's right," Kevin added. "We really don't have a choice. What do you think they want us to do?" His question was directed at Michael.

The four students talked over one another.

"Find the scrolls."

"Hide the scrolls."

"Kill someone." The last statement came from Minda.

"Listen. There is something very serious going on here. Why would they ask the four of us relatively innocent and untrained students to take on whatever it is they want. Let's just wait until we hear what Master Chan Wu has to say and then decide," Michael suggested.

"This is not a group decision, Michael. My sister and I will decide for ourselves. You and Kevin can make your own decisions." Minda was having none of the team approach.

Master Chan Wu and his daughter suddenly appeared back to the table. They had overheard the students arguing.

"Miss Temne, you must change your attitude about this. Among the four of you, there is no one who gets to decide alone. You all must agree or you all will be banished. Do you understand?" Ai Su Wu left them no way out. She sat down next to her father.

Master Chan Wu then shared with them the history of the scrolls.

"These scrolls contain all of the instructions and secret trainings used by every spirit of the wind and the woods. They had been recorded during a congress held long before humans began recording their own history. The congress was called because it was becoming clear to the spirit world that humankind would, if left to their own devices, bring chaos and disharmony into the world. It would be up to the spirit world to protect the Earth. They would have to do it cooperatively. It was vitally important that each tribe of spirits shared their powers with all the others in case one of the tribes was annihilated as a result of human activity. An agreement was reached where each tribe submitted a single scroll that contained all their secrets. Those scrolls were then entrusted to a group of three: a wood fairy, a kelpie, and a pixie. A dragon was also assigned to them as a protector. This worked for many eons until a dark tribe rose up in the Western Quarters. No one knew how long they had resided there.

"One night, the tribe from the Western Quarter invaded the sanctuary where the scrolls were kept hidden in a secret chamber. They killed the dragon and the kelpie, tortured the pixie, but the fairy escaped. The fairy sounded the alarm and legions of spirits flew to the sanctuary to repel the invaders. But they arrived too late. The pixie was dead. Fortunately, the secret location of the scrolls was not discovered. New protectors were assigned: a troll, an ogre, and a giant. They took the scrolls to a new location. Meanwhile, the western invaders seemed to have disappeared. That turned out not to be true.

"Every few hundred years, they appeared again in search of the scrolls. Each time they have been repelled, the scrolls kept secure. Then in the Year 562, the western tribe returned in vast numbers. They waged war on the entire spirit world and nearly wiped them out. By then the scrolls were in the hands of different protectors. Together, they decided that the scrolls must be moved to different shores. Over the objections of some of the spirit tribes, a union was formed with Saint Brendan to relocate the spirits along with their scrolls.

"One of the goddesses from the south, Toki, heard rumors during her many visits to her kin in Ireland that Saint Brendan was a man of special providence. With the western tribe threatening, she proposed approaching Saint Brendan with a proposition. Of course, it would mean revealing themselves to mortals in a direct way. She persuaded the tribal leaders to approach him. She was assigned the task.

"On a warm spring afternoon while Saint Brendan was completing his prayers on a hillock near his monastery, Toki and two other fairies, one from Asia and one from the Arctic, revealed themselves to Saint Brendan. At first taken aback by their sudden appearance, he was soon put at ease by Toki. They spent the rest of the day together. She shared the history of the Faye while he listened attentively. She explained in detail the nature of their secrets, the importance of their presence to preserve balance in the world, and pleaded with him to come to their aid. He asked for a short time apart from them to contemplate what she revealed. He wandered over to a small clearing to pray. While we don't know what happened during his time in contemplation, he returned to Toki to announce he would do all he could. Again, we have no record of what happened next, except we know that where he was to sail was not revealed to him until the night before he was to depart.

"Nowhere in any of his writings does Saint Brendan mention why he made the decision to help. We only know that he did. What happened during the voyage is set forth in the final testament you have just read."

Master Chan Wu continued, "The woman described in the testament was Adena. She has passed on, but her great-great-great-granddaughter, also named Adena, has succeeded her as Queen of the Western Quarter. She is fierce and bloodthirsty. Both Adenas have stopped at nothing over the ages to steal the scrolls. That is what the first Adena accomplished and is described in the final testament. Fortunately, a thousand years later, the other spirits under the leadership of a grogoch named Sproal laid siege to the western tribe and recaptured the scrolls. Once secured back with the protectors, the decision was made to fully entrust the scrolls to humans. Thirteen families were chosen by the fairy tribes to work together to preserve the scrolls. These thirteen families had long histories of belief in the spirit world. At one time or another, these families had contact with one or more of the tribes, although much of that history had been lost to them. Once selected, they were met by an emissary from the Faye. They were informed why they had been selected and what would be expected of them. Each of these families was also charged by the spirits to both protect the scrolls and to teach the secrets of the scrolls to their children so that if the scrolls were ever lost again, their secrets would not be."

"But why humans?" Michael asked.

Ai Su Wu explained this to the four students with a hint of sadness in her voice. "Because the spirit world was shrinking in number. Their traditional grounds were being overrun. Their ability to maintain the world in balance and harmony was waning. They believed that if humans could learn their secrets and cherish them as the spirits did, then there was hope for both worlds."

Master Chan Wu spoke again, "As you know, you are among the descendants of those first thirteen families. They formed the Clonfert Compact with the fairies to fulfill the promises they made to the spirits. Now, it is your turn to make good on the assurances given by your ancestors all those centuries ago."

Each of the four students knew that they were in the Saint Brendan's system because they possessed unique talents that most people would never understand. They also knew that they came from a long line of people known as 'enchanters.' However, they had no idea of their true history. It was always something of a mystery.

What wasn't mysterious was what was expected of them.

"So what do you want from us?" Affey asked.

"Adena is on the move again. We believe she is assembling a horde to seek the scrolls once more," Ai Su Wu said. "We just don't know how serious she is, or when she might strike."

"But why? Didn't they learn the secrets or make copies of the scrolls when they had them?" Kevin asked the question they were all thinking.

"That's the most interesting part of the history." The master smiled broadly. "They couldn't figure out how to read them. They never thought to copy them, I guess. They tried capturing various spirits over the centuries. They tortured them to no avail. Each one they captured refused to interpret the scrolls. However, we are concerned that they have someone now who can read them and that is why they are on the move again."

"So," Minda said, "what do you want us to do exactly?"

"It's rather simple to say, but difficult to do. You will defend the scrolls against the western tribe." Master Chan Wu turned to his daughter and whispered something to her. She left the table.

"You are all leaving in the morning for Clonfert House. Your parents have been told that you are going. While we did not share with them precisely why, they know, as descendants of the thirteen original families, that there are circumstances when the requests from the magisterium must be obeyed. You will not be returning to your homes tonight. You will remain here. In the morning, you will be taken to Clonfert House. You will be given time to make a phone call your parents, but you are to make no mention of what you have learned tonight or of the task you have been given. Your parents were told you have been selected to go to Clonfert House for special training, which is not a lie. My daughter will be back shortly to show you to your rooms. I must go to make the final arrangements with the magisterium. I will see you in the morning." With that, the master left.

After talking to their parents, the four students drifted off into a fitful sleep. The shared a common dream. The raven-haired woman from the final testament, Adena, kept sneaking into their dreams. She never said anything. She just stared at them. They all woke up several times, shaking. Eventually, they all fell soundly asleep. Michael woke up to Kevin pounding on his door.

Chapter Three

Enniskellin, Ireland
Saint Brendan's Academy
Leaving for Clonfert House

"Come on, Michael, you overslept. Master Chan Wu is agitated with you!" Kevin burst through Michael's door without knocking. He went straight to the clothes Michael left hanging over the chair and threw them at him. "Get dressed!" Kevin slammed the door behind him as he left.

Michael dressed as fast as he could and then headed to the dining room. He was the last one to arrive.

"Perhaps when you get to Clonfert House, you will be more mindful of the hours and get up on time." Master Chan was not too pleased with Michael this morning. Minda grinned at him. She liked the idea that his stature with the master had diminished.

Ai Su Wu was also there. She was carrying four small duffel bags.

"Your names are on the bag that is for you. There are clothes and toiletries for a few days. When you get to Clonfert House, they will provide you with the rest of what you need."

"Pardon me, miss, but I have special things that I use for my skin. I don't use ordinary soaps and lotions and neither does my sister," Minda said.

Master Chan Wu's patience with Minda was wearing thin. "You will use what you are provided." As he usually did when he wanted a point to sink in, he stared at her to make sure she understood.

"Yes, master. Sorry." It was Michael's turn to grin at Minda.

"The helicopter will be here shortly. In the meantime, please sit down and eat something while I provide you a few instructions that will help you when you arrive at Clonfert House."

Master Chan Wu then explained to the four students that, upon arrival, they would be met by a senior student named Gianni Giannotti. He would be the one who would make sure they got to the right place. He was also going to be their advisor for the rules of conduct at Clonfert House. "You may find him a bit flamboyant, but he knows the rules perfectly." The master informed them that they should expect little contact with the senior students at Clonfert House. They were to remember that these students had all been personally selected by the magisterium to undertake advanced, esoteric studies. They were the most elite among the students. The four should expect the senior students to treat them as a nuisance. The same would be true of the professors they might encounter. The professors were known to be aloof and unapproachable even by the finest of students. Should any of them encounter a professor, they were to step aside, cast their eyes downward, and utter not a word.

"You will initially be assigned to Professor Seamus O'Riley, the librarian. He will serve as your proctor, which means that he will be responsible for overseeing every aspect of your time at Clonfert House. He was part of the committee that chose the four of you." Master Chan Wu showed them a picture of Professor O'Riley on his cellphone. If the first impression of the professor tuned out to be true, then he was a big man. He would be very strong and intimidating. Master Chan Wu continued.

"Professor O'Riley is rough around the edges. He can sometimes seem angry, but he is not. I've known him for quite a long time and I have never seen him angry. What you will discover about him is that he takes things very seriously. He is also extremely suspicious, which made him the ideal person to proctor the four of you."

The master further explained that each of them would have an individual mentor. Minda's mentor would be Professor Tasha Mbaye, who was from Senegal. Her expertise was in the science of choice planting. She also was a mystic who regularly communicated with spirits. Affey was assigned to Professor Fritz Howenstein, a master of music, trigonometry, and confusion implementation. Kevin, the master explained, was a difficult one to place, although he didn't say why. The magisterium ultimately decided Professor Beatrice Smiley, Deputy Head of House and Department Chair of Transcendental Movement for him. Master Chan said that he only had a passing acquaintance with her, but she had a reputation for being bookish. Her usual response to just about everything was, "No." Unfortunately, Kevin's Uncle Finnean was away on assignment and would probably not return before the students' tasks were completed. Professor Anna Caracova was assigned to Michael. Master Chan Wu told Michael that she was a longtime friend of his. At times, he told Michael, she could be enigmatic, but she was, in his opinion, the most accomplished enchanter he had ever met. Her area of expertise was esoteric enhancement. Michael had no idea what that was. Michael informed that his Aunt Sheila was also away on magisterium business.

"Are there any questions?" Master Chan Wu asked.

Of course, Minda had to have at least one. "What if we don't like our mentor? Or, maybe I should say, what if they don't like us?"

Ai Su Wu intervened. She must have sensed that Minda was about to be admonished again by the master.

"There is no liking or disliking. From now on, there is only learning and doing. If you think of liking or disliking, you will fail. It is that simple."

"Does that answer your questions, Miss Temne?" Master Chan Wu asked her.

"Yes, master, it does. Thank you." She lowered her head so they couldn't see her face. Michael wondered if she really understood.

Kevin said, "I have a question, master. How long is all of this going to take? I mean, when do you think we will be coming back home?"

"Ah, a good question, but one that has no answer. You must focus on your task and the rest, including your return, will take care of itself. I think I hear the helicopter." Master Chan Wu stood and started out. They all followed him quickly, bags in hand, anxieties hidden.

Just before they boarded the helicopter, Master Chan Wu gathered them around him.

"Should you need to, and only if it is an extreme emergency, you are to use these." He handed each one of them a small, round black disc. It was about the size of a quarter. There was a flat button on one side. "You must keep these to yourselves. No one, and I mean no one, is to know you have these. If you are in extreme circumstances with no possibility of escape, then push the button. You will be rescued. Put them away before someone sees them. Guard them carefully. In the wrong hands, they could spell disaster."

They slipped the discs into their pockets. Minda asked, "What will happen if we use them?"

"Let's just hope you don't," answered Ai Su Wu.

"Now, off with you. I will hold you in my intentions until you return. I will keep watch over you from afar. Everything now depends on the four of you." Master Chan Wu then gestured that they should board.

The stairway to the helicopter descended and two young people, a boy and a girl in their twenties, stood at the bottom, flanking the stairs. As the four students cautiously approached, the two figures stepped forward to take their duffel bags.

"Welcome to Clonfert House," they said in unison. Within minutes, they were in the air heading over the green fields towards Galway. Michael watched out the window as Master Chan Wu's house, his house, Kevin's house, and all of Enniskellin faded away. The others did the same. Each wondered, 'When would I see my father again? When would I feel my mother's arms around me once more? How would my younger sister or brother be without me?' Just as Enniskellin was about to disappear, Michael swore he heard his grandmother, Siobhan, say, "This is what we do for them. This is why we were born. You are a Tynan. Bravery, cunningness, and strength run in your blood. Don't be afraid. The ancestors are with you."

Chapter Four

The Western Quarter
Adena's Council Chambers

Adena had sent word that the heads of all of the spirit tribes in the western quarter were to gather at the Mirror Pool on the night of the next new moon which was to occur in five days. She made it known that anyone who did not attend would be dealt with harshly. In the meantime, she called together her three most trusted generals to tell them what she had done in preparation to steal the scrolls from Clonfert House.

First to arrive for this meeting was General Ah Puch, a desert ogre and chief of the tribes of the underworld. He was followed shortly by the arrival of General Votan, a cliff dwelling ogre and architect of warfare. The last to arrive was General Cabrakan, a sky ogre and earthquake maker. He was accompanied by two animal spirits, Uncle Rabbit, the trickster and Sesimite, the shape-shifter.

"What is the urgency?" General Cabrakan asked General Ah Puch.

"Something about the scrolls at Clonfert House, I think. I've heard rumors that she has some new scheme to steal them," General Ah Puch said as he adjusted the two spears that crisscrossed his back.

Uncle Rabbit stepped between the two strong generals and explained, "I know what she has done." General Cabrakan kicked him aside.

Two manticores slithered into the hall and perched next to Adena's throne on the raised platform at the end of the hall. They signaled that she was about to arrive. The five cohorts assembled around the throne. Adena entered, dressed all in crimson, her black eyes flashing.

"Please," she began as she sat, "be seated." She waited for them to take their seats.

"I have great news. After all these eons, we now have the means and opportunity to strike Clonfert House, seize the scrolls, and regain what is rightfully ours. When we have succeeded, every earthly and heavenly power shall be ours."

"How? What have you done that makes this possible when we have failed so many times before?" General Votan, who had led so many of the former attempts to steal the scrolls and whose legions suffered tremendous losses, sounded skeptical. Adena was not pleased with his question.

"General Votan, you most of all should know that I would not be asking us to wage a war again if I wasn't certain of the outcome. Trust me. This time, we will not fail."

Sesimite, the shape-shifter who only spoke in howls when in the shape of a giant, let out a long piercing scream of excitement. Uncle Rabbit hid behind General Votan.

General Ah Puch took a step towards Adena, bent down on one knee, and then stood up directly in front of her.

"If you are this convinced, then we will all unite behind you. However, madam, I, for one, need to know how this is possible. I mean no disrespect, but if we are to once again put our legions at risk, it is only right that you tell us what you have set in motion. I fear that my tribe will be reluctant to go unless I can assure them that this time will be different. Our last encroachment against Clonfert House cost us dearly. It took more than a century for our numbers to rebound. So please, tell us what you have done so that we can stand before our men and women with confidence."

"I have to agree with General Votan, madam," said General Cabrakan. Uncle rabbit peeked out from behind General Votan to nod 'me too.'

"Yes, you must know. I intended to share this with you." Adena proceeded to explain why this time would be different.

It had come to her attention that the northern spirits had long ago decided to intermingle with the spirit tribes of the southern and eastern quarters. As a result, she thought, the blood loyalty of all of those three tribes had been diluted. What she believed had happened was that the intermingling of the tribal blood had created a fatal flaw in some of the spirits. Sometime later, the spirits undertook the most heinous course of action. They entrusted the scrolls to humans. They should have known that, instead of defending the scrolls without reservation or hesitation, they would eventually use the power of them only to serve their own interests. It was a defect of the human character that those spirits failed to account for. While generations of humans, specifically those who formed the Clonfert Compact, had acted in accordance with its terms, there were a few renegades who cared more about the power than the Compact. After much clandestine searching, she discovered that she was right. Although the existence of these renegade humans was extremely rare, she found two that she could approach. One of them, Jerome, had defected to join her household, though confined in a different realm. The other renegade remained at Clonfert House and was in regular contact with her through Jerome.

"Surely, the masters at Clonfert House are aware of what you found. And they must know of the defect." General Votan's tone was cautious.

"Yes, they know of the defect. In the past, they have known the names of those few who carry it, but not always. I believe that they do not know that we have two of them in our ranks," Adena said.

"What about the one traitor who you say is in contact with you?" asked Uncle Rabbit.

Adena was anxious to answer because she had devised a clever plan to throw Clonfert House off.

"We delivered an urn of ashes to Clonfert House with a letter explaining to them that this was the first of the dead student's remains. We would bring them if they did not enter into negotiations with us to share the knowledge of the scrolls. We included in the ashes the charms this defector wore around his neck. As you all know, when these enchanters reach the highest levels of achievement, they wear a charm that identifies them as advanced practitioners. Obviously, we have not had a response from Clonfert House, so we must now prepare to advance on them."

"How do you know that their failure to respond is not some sort of a trap? These humans are powerful now that they possess the knowledge of the scrolls." General Cabrakan was not convinced.

"Our defector at Clonfert House recently informed us that four minor enchanters from one of the lesser academies have been summoned to train for some secret undertaking. Only a few at Clonfert House know what that mission might be. What our defector has been able to learn is that these four, in combination, are said to hold all of the powers detailed in the scrolls. Only once before has all the power been so closely aligned." Adena then shared a secret part of her past.

Adena had once been the western quarters' envoy to Clonfert House, a position now eliminated. While serving in that capacity, she gained access to some of the documents in the recesses of the library. In these documents were the details of the history of all of the spirit tribes. Her hosts at Clonfert House had no objections to her use of the library until she discovered the *Liber Secreto of Finbar Mag Aedha*. In that book, she learned of a secret voyage that removed the spirits and their scrolls to an unknown location across the sea. She also read of an encounter the author had with her great-great-grandmother, also named Adena. It was her great-great-grandmother who had first come into possession of the scrolls. But what struck her the most was that it appeared that the scrolls described powers beyond those possessed by her tribe. Later during her studies, she would learn that while many of the enchanting powers were shared among the tribes, each had special enchantments that only they had. Not one tribe possessed all the powers. The scrolls mentioned in the *Liber Secreto* held the key to unifying all the powers in one tribe. She needed to find them and take possession of the scrolls and their powers. She heard someone approaching, so she quickly placed the book back to where she found it. She slid back between the stacks to hide until she was alone again.

When she returned to retrieve the book so she could finish reading it, she came upon a ledger that was marked, *'Initial Breedings.'* There, she discovered a list of the first pairings between spirits of the various quarters and the names of their offspring, together with some prediction of their particular power. Her name was on that list. Her parents were a water nymph from the north and one of the nine sons of the Dragon King of the east. It was predicted that she would gain all the powers of enchantment except one. What that one power might be was not listed. As she sat there taking stock of what this might mean, the librarian, a hulk of a man, found her. She was immediately placed in chains and summoned before the high council. Without any opportunity to defend herself, she was stripped of her credentials. She was brought before two masters who attempted to erase her memory. She was able to fake the result they were seeking. She was banished back to the western quarter. Later, she was able to figure out that while her powers had in fact been greatly diminished, the only power she lacked was clairvoyance. She did not tell the generals about this. She knew it would put her at a disadvantage. It was her one and only weakness, a weakness that would keep her from success.

"Now you know my history. Keep it to yourselves. Just know that I am not to be trifled with. Go. Gather your legions. We will assemble here in one week. That will give you sufficient time to get your hordes in order and to make provisions for those left behind." She rose from her seat, the manticores slithered out before her and she departed, her dark robes trailing behind like ghosts. The three generals, Uncle Rabbit, and Sesimite waited out of respect until she was clear of her chambers.

"I think that before we each go our separate ways to prepare, we should talk about what we just heard," General Ah Puch said.

"I agree. But not here." General Votan suggested they travel a few miles away to an inn where he knew the proprietress. They could talk safely there.

Chapter Five

The Western Quarter
The Inn of Jaguar

The three ogre generals and the two animal spirits sat at a table in the darkest corner of the inn. There, away from prying eyes and sharp ears, they could speak openly. The proprietress, Flavia Maricruz, a jaguar spirit, kept watch for any suspicious persons. General Votan was on edge.

"I don't like this," he said as he checked over his shoulder to make sure no one was close enough to overhear them. "Every time she has sent us out in the past, she has come up with a story about how this time would be different. If she had the history with the Clonfert House she talked about, then how come she didn't tell us before? I don't trust her."

"What choice do we have, Votan?" asked General Ah Puch. "We have sworn to follow her."

"Yes, but only if what she is doing is for the good of us all. Is that what she is doing now, or is this about her getting revenge?" General Votan replied.

They all sat quietly for a few minutes. Then General Cabrakan suggested that they try to find out who the two

Clonfert House traitors were. "We need to know this," he said, "because we have to try to figure out if they are really on our side or if they might be decoys planted by Clonfert House."

Sesimite uttered a low growl and banged hard on the table.

"What's your problem?" General Votan never really cared for Sesimite. General Votan thought that shape-shifters were a certain breed of cowards to be avoided. Sisemite growled lower and more intensely at General Votan, who ignored him.

General Ah-Push next raised a concern about the four novice enchanters who had been summoned to Clonfert House. If they really did have the perfect combination of powers between them and if they could learn to harness those powers, then how could they possibly defeat them? General Cabrakan expressed his concern about them also. Another silence fell over them.

"I can find out," Uncle Rabbit offered. "Of all of us, I am the only one small enough and crafty enough to go undetected. What if I go to Clonfert House?"

"We already have someone there according to Adena," said General Ah Puch.

General Votan added, "But what if they are really working for Clonfert House and not us? Perhaps they have been planted to ensnare us by providing false information?" If the traitor was false, they needed to know.

"Just leave it to me," said Uncle Rabbit, a bit overconfident. "I can leave at once and see what I can see. If this traitor is legitimate, then I will find out."

They argued back and forth about the merits of Uncle Rabbit's plan. The one obstacle that they all identified as his biggest challenge was not gaining entrance to Clonfert House but finding out who the traitor was. General Cabrakan suggested they try to pry the information out of Adena. Chances of that being successful, all agreed, were remote, unless Uncle Rabbit was willing to infiltrate her encampment.

"Oh, I don't know about that," Uncle Rabbit said, shrinking back against his chair. "If she's as powerful as she says she is, she will see me immediately. You all know that my punishment would be death."

"Then what other options do we have? The only way for us to determine if we should follow her this time rests on our ability to take the measure of these supposed traitors." General Votan was digging in. "Let Uncle Rabbit go. At least there's a possibility he will discover something of use for us. In the meantime, the rest of us will try to find out who the defector is that is lodged with Adena. Are we all agreed?" Each answered that they were. Sisemite growled.

Before he left, Uncle Rabbit persuaded the others to allow Sesimite to travel with him. Sesimite had one other ability that he really used; he could appear as anything that was alive. There would certainly be opportunities for him to use those skills to assist Uncle Rabbit. Again, they all agreed. Uncle Rabbit and Sisemite immediately departed for Clonfert House. As spirits, they could make the journey from the western quarter in just a single day.

Chapter Six

The Western Quarter
Inside Adena's Chambers

Adena's mood was growing darker. Despite her efforts to convince the three tribal generals that she had a fool-proof plan, she knew them well enough to know that they would probably meet together to determine if what she said was true. She knew that her experience as the envoy to Clonfert House would be easy enough to discover. All they had to do was confirm that with the archivist. No doubt, the archivist would confirm her appointment and say nothing more. Her oath as archivist forbade her from divulging details of any record. She could only confirm dates and places. If she could reveal what happened during Adena's time at Clonfert House, they would learn that she was stripped of more of her powers than she admitted to the generals. She could no longer thought-project or dislocate. Her power to thought-bend was severely diminished, and her ability to move freely between the spirit and human worlds was fraught with obstacles which meant she could never set foot in Clonfert House herself. This left her with only the power to implement confusion. Even this power was only a fraction of what it once was. Now, she had become entirely dependent of those she handpicked to surround her. Even they were not privy to her limited abilities. There were, however, two non-enchanter powers she possessed that served her quite well.

First was the power of her blood-thirsty reputation, especially when it came to all matters related to the scrolls. Second, she had a tongue that could persuade even the most skeptical to her way of thinking. It was this latter skill that she had come to rely on more and more as her obsession with the scrolls grew.

There was one secret she kept from everyone. It was one that would make discovery of the defector from Clonfert House impossible to detect. It was a power that had not yet risen in her when she was dismissed as envoy and stripped of her powers. She could appear in human form, but only in a realm apart from both the human and spirit worlds. In the annuls of the spirit world, there were less than fifteen cases of this ability. As far as she knew, she was the only one still alive with this ability. She closed her eyes, sat motionless, and transformed.

She transported herself to another dimension where humans were kept apart from their own kind and the spirit world because they had abandoned their ancestors in search of riches. The spirits assigned to this realm were able to fulfill those wishes while at the same time manipulating the humans into service. It was a realm open to only a small cadre of spirits. It was in this realm that the defector from Clonfert House was kept.

"Fetch me Jerome," she said as she materialized in this hidden realm. A woman of indeterminate age bowed her head and scurried off to find Jerome.

Jerome was pushed through the tent's opening. He kneeled before Adena, trembling. "Madam Adena, I'm surprised to see you. I don't have any new information for you. As we agreed, when I have something to report to you, I will dispatch a messenger to inform you."

"That is the problem, Jerome," she said tersely. "I expect more from you and your colleague at Clonfert House. Is there some obstacle in your communicating with her that I am not aware of, or are the two of you growing too comfortable with our arrangements?"

"No, madam, we are all too aware of our responsibilities. It is just that things have grown quiet there. The four young students I reported about recently appear to have settled into a schedule of routine study, although a little advanced for them, given their ages."

"There must be more to it than that. I know how devious those professors can be. The headmaster, Boru, is a clever one. He is the most accomplished magus. Find out what is really going on, or you and your cohort will suffer my wrath. Do I make myself clear?" As she spoke, she grabbed him by the chin, pulled his face up closer to hers, and squeezed hard. When she finally released him, her fingerprints were embedded on his cheeks. "I will return tomorrow. There better be more from you." Then she vanished.

Jerome went straight to his room. He was sweating profusely. He had never felt as afraid as he did at that moment. He rang for a messenger who he instructed to make their way to Clonfert House. This sprite went to inform his colleague at Clonfert House that within twenty-four hours, he must have more information. If not, they were both going to probably be delivered to the hands of the magisterium as traitors. The messenger took wing. There was nothing more for Jerome to do, but to wait. For the rest of the day, he kept to his room. Several times, he thought of returning to the magisterium, confessing his misdeeds, and asking for mercy. But he had no idea how to get away from the realm where he was being kept. The despair he felt was smothering him. Why, he asked himself over and over, had he betrayed the very people he had sworn to protect just as generations of his family had done for almost a thousand years. He was ashamed of himself. He no longer had any control over his destiny.

Chapter Seven

Galway, Ireland
Arrival at Clonfert House

Unless one was selected as a student, one was not permitted to enter Clonfert House. It was an invisible estate. It could only be seen by those who were invited by the magisterium to enter into its mysteries. It surrounded Saint Brendan's Cathedral, yet remained invisible to the thousands of visitors to the cathedral. Clonfert House was built as a fortress to protect not just the cathedral but Clonfert House itself. When the Clonfert Compact was signed, each of the spirit tribes from the four quarters sent their most accomplished artisans to construct Clonfert House. Until its completion, not a single human being could see it or feel its presence. The day after it was completed, the thirteen founding families were invited to a ceremony in the cathedral led by the Korean spirit, Hananim. Representatives from each of the tribes of the four quarters were present. During the ceremony, each of the members of the families was initiated into the spells, incantations, and charms that made entry into its halls possible. As the final charm was cast, they heard that the wind howled and lightning struck. Rain pelted the cathedral. Inside, the candles flickered and then went out. From the transept, a glow rose from the floor. The golden light slowly illuminated the cathedral. As it grew brighter, the thirteen families saw that only Hananim remained. All the other spirits were gone.

"Your time has come, my dear friends, for you to step into Clonfert House. What you will see must remain our secret. You must never divulge how you enter or what is inside," Hananim instructed them

A voice called out to him, "How is it that pilgrims coming to the cathedral can't see it?"

Hananim then explained, "We have placed a spell two miles outside the city. Anyone inside the two-mile radius is blind to the existence of Clonfert House. All of you were under that spell when you arrived." This last comment created a murmur through the cathedral. "As a secondary precaution, you no doubt noticed the wall surrounding the cathedral. You all have entered here through the one and only portal, i.e. through the wall. Once you leave here tonight, we will cast another spell around the portal as a precaution."

Then he led them through the apse and to a rear wall behind the sanctuary. He placed his left hand on the wall, muttered something no one could hear, and the wall swung open to reveal a long, candle-lit corridor. "Welcome to Clonfert House." He plucked one of the torches on the wall near the entrance and led them on a tour of Clonfert House. This was the one and only time any member of the original thirteen families was permitted entrance to Clonfert House. From tomorrow onward, only those invited to reside there were permitted to enter. All those invited would be their descendants.

*

As the helicopter approached Clonfert House, one of the flight crew came back into the cabin and addressed the four students.

"We are now approaching Clonfert House. As you all know, this is hallowed ground. You have probably heard stories about Clonfert House. I am asking you to discard them all. Look out of the windows. What do you see?"

Michael and Kevin looked out of one window on the right side of the helicopter. Minda and Affey did the same on the left.

Minda said, "I see in the distance the Cathedral of Saint Brendan. It looks like a line of pilgrims at its gate, but I don't see Clonfert House."

"One rumor you may have heard is true. Clonfert House is invisible to all but those invited to reside there. There is a spell cast across the area that protects its invisibility. It also makes our approach invisible as well. Now, please prepare to land."

Once the attendant had returned to her seat, Minda turned to Michael. "Did you know about this invisibility?"

"I heard the rumors, but didn't pay it much attention."

"Kevin?" she asked.

"Same here. And you and your sister? Did you know?" Kevin asked.

Minda saw this as an opportunity to establish a position superior to the others. "Of course, I and my sister knew.

Anyone with half a brain would believe of the magic of Clonfert House," she lied.

No sooner did she finish her sentence than the helicopter entered a steep bank, pushing each of them tight against the back of their seats. It then evened out and gently landed.

The helicopter set down in front of the now-visible granite mansion that served as the central administration building at Clonfert House. Michael and Kevin looked out the window on the left side of the helicopter and saw a short, squat raven-haired young man waving frantically. Minda leaned across to see what Michael and Kevin were looking at.

"Isn't he a sight?" she said with a chuckle. Affey seemed lost in her thoughts.

The young man they were looking at was dressed in what they assumed was the Clonfert House's uniform—baggy gray pants, matching three-quarter-length jacket tied at the waist, no buttons, and starched-white shirt underneath. He also was wearing a lavender scarf around his neck that was flapping wildly from the whirl of the helicopter blades.

"This must be Gianni Giannotti," Kevin said.

The male crew member went to open the hatch. The stairs unfolded onto the emerald-green lawn. He secured the stairs in place and then gestured for the four of them to disembark. Minda grabbed Affey by the hand and charged down the stairs. Michael and Kevin sprang up to follow them. Minda and Affey had made it almost to Gianni Giannotti's open arms.

"Buon giorno, buon giorno, i miei amici!" Gianni was shouting over the helicopter noise, with his arms wide as if he was trying to embrace all of them at once.

"Ah, Miss Minda and Miss Affey," he said as he kissed them lightly on the back of their hands. Minda pulled hers away and rubbed it on her pants. Affey didn't seem to know how to react.

"Mr. O'Connell," he said formally to Kevin as he extended his hand. Kevin gave Michael a quick look and shook Gianni's hand vigorously. He was not sure why he did that.

"Mr. Tynan," he addressed Michael as if he were some newfound relic. "I am most pleased to meet you." He emphasized the 'you,' which prompted Minda to glare at Michael. Gianni stood absolutely still for a moment as if he had forgotten something. Then, having figured out what it was, he continued.

"My friends, for now all of you are my new friends. You know that is a fact. Let us introduce you to Clonfert House. You are fortunate indeed to be admitted here without having to have gone through the usual channels." As he talked, he walked briskly ahead of them, shouting his words over his shoulder.

"Tell me," he said as they made their way to the entrance of the administration hall, "why are you here? This is most unusual." The way he asked the question hinted that he may know the answer to his question. None of them said a word. He stopped on the top step, his hand on the heavy doorknob. "Well?" He was still hoping one of them would say something.

Minda spoke up. "The way of our visit is none of your concern. Perhaps your question is better asked of the Professor O'Riley." She fixed him with her blue eyes.

"Is that how it's going to be with you? How about the rest of you?" Gianni was not hiding either his annoyance or his arrogance. Again, the four of them remained silent.

"Very well." He continued as if nothing was remiss, "Let us show you to your rooms, then off to meet with Professor Seamus O'Riley. I'm sure you've heard all about him." This last comment about Professor O'Riley was presented to them as something of a warning.

Gianni led the four students through the expanse of the entry of the administration building and up a dual winding staircase up to what appeared to them to be the fourth floor. It was difficult to tell just how far they climbed because the staircase took a series of odd turns. Sometimes the stairs seemed to be taking them back down when suddenly they could look down only to discover that they were actually higher than just a second before. It was very confusing for each of them as much of Clonfert House would turn out to be. Affey seemed to be particularly agitated by it all.

When they reached the floor where they were to reside, Gianni stopped ceremoniously on the landing. His tone turned serious. His demeanor became more formal. "No one else lives up here. It will be just the four of you. All the other students live on the far side of the campus. Because of this, you will have little, if any, contact with them. You will take your meals in the general refectory where we all take our meals, but you be seated at your own table. I will join you from time to time. Now, to your rooms. First, the ladies." He bowed to them and led them down the hallway to the right of the landing. They disappeared around a corner.

"I don't like this guy," Kevin said. "I think he's kind of snarky, especially with the girls."

"Jealous?" Michael asked.

"Of him! You must be kidding." Kevin rejected Michael's suggestion, but the way he reacted hinted that there was a least a hint of concern that Affey might find Gianni a distraction. Despite his protests, Kevin harbored a keen interest in Affey. It wasn't exactly romantic, but it was more than friendship.

"He seems harmless enough. I just think he's being who he is. You know how the Italians can be. Remember Enzo, the boy from Abruzzo who only lasted two years? He was the friendliest, most gregarious boy at school. He was a hit with the girls, but he was harmless." Michael tried to reassure Kevin. Michael knew of Kevin's blossoming infatuation with Affey.

"Yeah, until the Korean kid called him out one day and he blew up." Kevin reminded Michael that Enzo's temper could flare up and when it did, you hoped you weren't in his sights. His quick temper would eventually lead to his dismissal. He waited almost three months to get back at the Korean boy. He sucker-punched him and broke his nose. Enzo was gone by dinnertime.

"Gentlemen!" Gianni shouted from the far end of the hallway. "Now to your rooms." He led Michael and Kevin to the left of the landing. The landing marked the boundary between men and women on this floor.

He led them down the hallway, around two corners, and eventually to what must be the last rooms on that side of the hallway.

"Mr. O'Connell, you are in here." He motioned for Kevin to enter Room Number Thirty-Six.

"Mr. Tynan, here." He pointed to the room opposite Kevin's, which for some odd reason was Number One Hundred and Seventy-Four. "I will meet you back on the landing in fifteen minutes. Take this time to unpack your things and change into the uniforms that have been placed on your beds. You must wear these uniforms at all times unless you leave the campus. Then you can wear whatever you like, except you may not wear the uniform off campus. It would arouse suspicion and confuse the pilgrims. Fifteen minutes!" He stepped lively down the hallway.

"I half thought he was going to skip," Kevin remarked.

Michael's room was bigger than any room in his house in Enniskellin. At the academy, he shared a room a quarter this size with three other students, including Kevin. The ceiling was at least twelve feet high. The wall opposite the door was almost entirely window. There was a fireplace opposite the four-poster bed. The room was bright and dark at the same time. It felt warm and inviting. Yet, something felt unsettled at the same time. There was a private bath, something else Michael had never had in his whole life. Laid out on the bed were three uniforms. On the floor were two pair of shoes, one black and one brown, and a pair of blue and white sneakers. Inside the closet were a raincoat, a light windbreaker, a heavy woolen cape, and a wool-knitted hat. Everything was the same color of ash-gray. His dresser contained seven sets of underwear, all gray, and fourteen pair of socks, also gray. Gray was a theme. The bathroom was brilliantly white. There was soap, shampoo, and an assortment of toiletries. The administration had thought of everything. At least they had thought of everything gray. There was no TV. On the desk in the corner was a professional-grade Apple computer. There were no other electronics of any kind. On the desk was Michael's username and temporary password to sign on to the internet. There was a knock on the door. It was Kevin.

"If I didn't have a family, I'd never leave here," he said as he blasted into Michael's room. When he reached the windows, he stopped abruptly. "I have the same view out of my window. How can that be? I'm on the opposite side of the hallway." He rushed off towards his room. Michael rushed right behind him to see what he was talking about.

Kevin's room was freakishly identical to Michael's in each and every detail.

"Look, Michael. Look out my window. It's the same view as yours." Kevin was starting to get anxious, maybe even scared.

When Michael looked out, it was the same view from his window, except for one detail that Kevin missed. "You're right, Kevin. It is. But look again. It's a mirror image. Everything is the same, just reversed."

Kevin dashed back and forth between their rooms several times. "Wow! That's amazing. How do they do that?" He seemed more excited than anxious now. "We better change. It's almost time to meet back on the landing." Kevin started to change into his gray uniform. Michael returned to his room to do the same.

While Michael changed into his uniform, he couldn't help but wonder if the girls were having the same experience as Kevin and he were having. He wasn't sure how he felt about all of this—the sameness of everything, at least so far. Why was it like this? What was the lesson in all of this sameness, if there was one? He would just have to wait and see.

When Michael and Kevin arrived at the landing, Gianni was pacing and muttering to himself. He seemed angry.

"Where are the girls?" he said under his breath. He didn't want Michael and Kevin to hear him or see his displeasure with the girls. When he saw Michael and Kevin, he stopped pacing. He attempted to change his mood, though it didn't really work. "Gentlemen, we must hurry. Professor O'Riley says he wants to meet all of you as soon as possible. You will soon learn that you don't want to keep him waiting." Gianni started pacing again. "Where are those girls?"

Affey rounded the corner of the hallway alone.

"My sister says to tell you that she needs a little more time."

Gianni was out of patience. He snapped at Affey, "You go back and tell your sister that she must come NOW! Professor O'Riley wants to see all of you immediately. Tell her there will be consequences if she doesn't come NOW!" He was having trouble controlling his anger. Affey ran back down the hallway. They stood silently waiting for Minda. They didn't wait long.

"You must be more punctual if you are to make it here," Gianni said as he hurried down the stairs with all of them in tow. They expected a challenge from Minda, but she didn't say anything.

Once again, they were rushed down hallways, up and down several flights of stairs, around too many corners to remember, until at last they stopped in front of a huge double oak door. Two gargoyles were carved into it. The faced each other as if they were the sentries who were responsible for opening the doors.

"This is the door to the library and Professor O'Riley's study. You must knock only twice. Not once, not three or four times—twice. He won't respond to any other knock. Do you understand?" Gianni looked to each of them for a nod that they understood the two-knock protocol. He knocked on the door twice.

"Do you have the four of them with you? If not, come back when you do. And make it quick." The voice behind the doors was deep and gruff. It reminded Kevin of a wrestler he once saw at the circus. Affey took a step back from the door. Minda stepped forward as if she were going to respond when Gianni held up his hand to stop her.

"They are all here, professor." They all stood absolutely still, waiting for whatever was next.

Two or three minutes passed in silence. No one said a word, though Minda wanted to say something to break the silence. Even Gianni became remarkably still. When the door finally opened, Professor O'Riley stood in the threshold staring at them.

He was a mountain of a man. 'Yes,' Kevin thought. 'He must have been a wrestler when he was younger. Surely, no one would challenge him about anything.' His hair was short-cropped and gray. He had ice-blue eyes that twinkled in opposition to his bulk. His robe was the same simple ash-gray. There were no adornments.

"Well, you're young ones, aren't you?" He took his time looking each of them over. "Which one of you is Tynan?"

Michael didn't like being singled out. Minda didn't seem to like it either. "I am, sir."

"Humph." That was all Professor O'Riley said.

"Minda, I presume," he said, stepping in front of her.

"I am," she answered, not adding the 'sir' that he was surely expecting. Already she was staking out her territory.

"Affey. Kevin." He acknowledged them in turn.

"Thank you, Mr. Giannotti. That is all for now." He dismissed Gianni.

"Please, come in." He gestured for the four of them to enter his study. Minda took Affey by the hand. She was the first to enter the Professor's study.

This was the den of a scholar. Bookcases crammed with texts ancient and new. Scrolls stacked on tables, with curiosities strewn about. It all had a sense of organized chaos, the kind of chaos where the professor would know where everything was and would also know if something was missing or misplaced. He had the students sit around in a very round conference table in the middle of his study.

"Sit wherever you like," he said as he took his place at the table closest to his desk. From where he sat, he was framed by the enormous glass window that rose to the ceiling behind his desk. The light from the window surrounded him in an amber glow.

Then he asked the first question of many they would be asked in the days to come. "Do you know why we are sitting at a round table?"

"Because we're not at a square one," Minda said with a hint of defiance.

They others looked at the professor for his reaction. Affey tried to shrink into her chair and disappear.

"A bit sure of yourself, are you, Minda?" the professor began. "We will see just how confident you are when you are not protected by the walls of this house." He turned his attention to a folder in front of him.

As he opened the folder, he stopped and closed it. "Minda, please go through that door over there and make us all some tea. You'll find all you need on the counter. And, before you say anything, I'd take a moment to reflect." They all looked at her. She had no reaction at all. She stood up as if this was something she routinely did. She went directly through the door the professor indicated.

"You will all do well to remember your place in the order of things here. We will wait for Minda and the tea." He went to his desk where he signed several pieces of paper while they waited.

Kevin fidgeted. Affey kept looking towards the door behind which they could hear Minda placing cups on saucers. All each of them could think about was why they had been summoned here so quickly. They knew that some danger was rising. Master Chan Wu made it sound urgent and ominous. Professor Riley didn't seem rushed at all. In fact, he made them feel as if they were at Clonfert House, being interviewed for possible admission. Nothing about him suggested anything out of the ordinary. They were confused.

"Tea is ready," Minda announced as she pushed open the door and carried the tray of teapot and cups over to the table. "I found a tin of cookies on the shelf, so I brought some of those too, professor. Hope you don't mind." She had to stake out some territory.

"That's fine," he muttered as he returned to the table and sat down. "Please, help yourselves." He opened the file again.

"Here's a cup for you, professor," Minda said as she passed it to Affey so she could pass it on to the professor.

He didn't respond.

Once they all had a cup of tea and a cookie, he closed his eyes as if in deep contemplation. They sat watching him for several minutes without moving. Michael wondered if his suddenly turning quiet was for effect or for some health reason.

"Now," he said as if he hadn't drifted off, "let's review the rules for you while you are here. Here is a copy of your daily schedule. As you can see, we begin the day in quiet reflection, just as you have been used to at your academy. After breakfast, you will attend the classes listed at the times given. This will take you through noon. After the noon meal, you will come here for your afternoon assignments. Those assignments will vary depending on how you and the others are progressing."

"What others?" Minda said without skipping a beat. "Did you mean the others of us around the table, or are there others hidden somewhere else at Clonfert House?"

"Despite what Master Chan Wu may have told you, none of you is particularly extraordinary." He needed to put Minda in her place, but he didn't want to single her out for admonishment. "Yes, you have strong pedigrees and unusually advanced skills. All of you come from one of the founding families and have relatives in current positions of power. But the task ahead requires much more than the current level of your skills. This is true even though Master Chan Wu may have suggested otherwise. Others will be joining you if and when we decide your skills need to be supplemented. If we do, then you will meet them as they arrive. You four are a hope for us; that is all you are. And we all know that what we hope for doesn't always come to pass. Yes, Minda? Do you have a question?"

"I'm sure we all have questions, professor, but I for one would like to know precisely why we have been brought here and why we are not given a choice in this matter." Kevin admired her courage in saying something he wished he had said.

"That's a fair question. I am sure each of you would like to ask me that as well. Am I right?"

They all nodded.

"I'll just say this for now. The very thing your families swore to protect is about to come under siege. How we know this is for a later time. To combat what we fear is about to unfold, we need to bring together the best enchanters we can, even if they are still not settled in their skills. You and others have been identified as possessing the unusual level of skill we believe we will need if we are to succeed. After much debate, we arrived at the conclusion that you four had the most potential. But, as I said, we have others identified who can be brought in if needed. This is not the first time we have been faced with this potential calamity. We succeeded before and we will again. Starting tomorrow, we will begin to hone and strengthen your skills.

You will learn how to employ them alone and in concert with others. That is all you need to know for now."

Affey spoke up. "And if we fail?"

Professor O'Riley tried to put her at ease. "Affey, at this moment, we have no reason to believe you won't succeed. If we had any doubt, you wouldn't be here."

"But you have others in waiting." Affey's voice quivered.

"Only out of prudence. If you were in our shoes, you would have done the same. Now, let's get back to the task at hand."

"Professor," Michael interrupted, "why are we being kept apart from the others here?"

The professor sighed. "No matter how advanced one becomes in the practice of their skills, no matter how evolved one becomes in their personal growth, and no matter how distant one can move from notions of one's self, jealousy always seems to burrow in. Ego raises its ugly head. None of the advanced students in residence here was selected for this. When word gets out, there will be those who see you as a threat to their status and futures. My responsibility, as well as the responsibility of the other professors here, is to keep that in check. We must see that your work proceeds without interference. Sometimes, we may fail at this. It's a risk we must all take."

Affey sat up straighter in her chair as if she was going to say something.

"Yes, Affey?" the professor asked.

"What if we want to go home instead?" She couldn't look at him.

"You may, but I believe Master Chan Wu explained the consequences." The professor was abrupt with Affey. He knew he had to toughen her up, starting now.

He closed the folder and pushed back his chair. The first meeting with him was over.

"Before you go back to your rooms, let me give you some advice. Be careful who you talk with, especially anyone outside of your circle. Some are already aware you are here and being kept apart. They will, no doubt, hatch schemes to find out who you are and why you are here. All you need to tell them is that you have been sent here to study with me for a few weeks and then you are returning to your academies. Do not share any particulars with them. Should anyone push you to hard, then let me know. Gianni, who you've already become friends with is my most trusted advisee. He is clever and loyal. He knows every passage through and around the labyrinth that is Clonfert House. It is easy to become disoriented. He will guide you. Though he will serve you in that way, he will not inquire as to the reasons for your being here even though he already has. He was following my instructions. Your first test, which by the way you passed perfectly. He has been told not to ask again and to be discreet about sharing what he knows about you with the other students." He stood up and they all stood as well.

"Gianni is waiting for you outside the door. He will take you on a tour of our esteemed Clonfert House." He turned to his desk and the four of them started for the door. "Before you leave, please place the little devices Master Chan Wu gave you in the basket by the door. They won't work here unless I modify them. You will have them returned to you during our session tomorrow afternoon."

"How did he know about them?" Kevin whispered.

"There's very little I don't know," the professor said from the far side of the room.

"No secrets here," Minda said, making sure the professor heard her.

"Best to keep that in mind," he answered.

Affey opened the door. Gianni was there, arms outstretched to embrace them all once again. Soon enough, they would learn that this was just Gianni and he would not be denied a hug.

Chapter Eight

The Northern Quarter
At the Eo Mugna Tree
(The Sacred Ewe)

"Hurry up, Sesimite. We are already hours behind and you know how angry General Ah Puch and the other generals can get when things aren't moving along as planned."

"Hurumph!" was Sesimite's response to Uncle Rabbit's worried voice.

Sesimite wanted to stop and rest. He sat down under a large yew tree. Uncle Rabbit scurried back to him.

"We can't stop, Sesimite. We must keep moving."

Sesimite ignored Uncle Rabbit and stretched out on the ground.

What neither of them realized was that they had stopped under the Eo Mugna Tree. The Eo Mugna Tree was a legendary, mystical, sacred tree. It could feed a person and impart magical knowledge. It could instill ancient wisdom to those worthy of receiving it. It could also be an avenger against those who harmed others. Up in its branches and deep in its shadows lived the Green Maiden together with her guardians. Sesimite and Uncle Rabbit were about to meet them.

Sesimite reached up to the lowest branch and picked two apples and a handful of hazelnuts.

"Really, Sesimite, you're eating?" Uncle Rabbit's annoyance with Sesimite was fraying. But what could he do? Sesimite was an immovable object when he was eating. Uncle Rabbit had no choice but to be patient and wait for Sesimite to decide he was ready to move on. Uncle Rabbit sat down a short distance away from Sesimite to think about what lay ahead.

As the afternoon sun was rising higher in the sky, a rusting in the leaves above him made Sesimite stop eating. Uncle Rabbit turned towards the noise high up in the tree. There, moving down through the branches, were a company of spirits, or at least that was what Uncle Rabbit thought. They moved from limb to limb, snatching a hazelnut here or an apple there. They didn't seem to be aware that Uncle Rabbit and Sesimite were sitting below. However, Sesimite wasn't pleased with their arrival and he hurled an apple up into the tree.

"Hey, you down there. What do you think you are doing? We can come down there and bind you to this tree forever." The sprite, fairies, or pixies, or whatever they were, scampered down the branches until they were just about Sesimite's level. In the meantime, Uncle Rabbit had hidden himself behind a boulder. Sesimite was confused by their sudden appearance.

"And you, there behind the boulder. How'd you like to be chained to that rock forever? You're trespassing here. Our mistress won't appreciate it." This sprite seemed to be in charge of the others. Uncle Rabbit tried to figure out how many of them were up among the branches, but mostly he just heard them. Only this one who spoke was clearly visible.

Uncle Rabbit knew all about the Eo Mugna Tree. He knew the stories about how the tree could impart a great deal of knowledge if it deemed one worthy. But he thought it was just a myth. He had no idea that it actually existed. Yet, here he was beneath its branches. What confused him was why these wee folks were here. None of the stories he had heard mentioned creatures dwelling in the tree. None of the stories even hinted at a woman having anything to do with the Eo Mugna Tree. There was no reason for them to be climbing in the tree just for nuts and fruit. It bothered him that they seemed intent on chasing them away. He decided to come out from his hiding place and face them. They knew he was there anyway.

He puffed out his chest as he moved confidently toward to branches where several more of the little creatures were perched. He challenged them. "You may threaten us, but we're not afraid of you. We have powers beyond what you can comprehend. We can withstand any of your feeble attempts to conjure some trick to chase us off or hold us here."

"Is that so?" said the one with silver hair and beard, who seemed to be the elder of the group.

"Yes, it is," Uncle Rabbit said, sitting up on his hind legs to make himself look taller. As he did, the little creatures in the tree nearly tumbled out of the branches with laughter. Sesimite rose up to his full giant height. The troop of spirits in the branches stopped laughing. They moved to higher perches.

"Oh, my, my, my," said the silver-haired one. "You think the two of you scare us? You obviously don't know who we are, do you?" His blue eyes fixed first on Sesimite and then on Uncle Rabbit. Several minutes passed before Uncle Rabbit spoke. The leader of this tiny band of creatures was starting to scare Uncle Rabbit.

"Let me tell you something, you imp," Uncle Rabbit said, trying to stand even taller. Sesimite moved behind him and growled. "We come from the west. We have vast armies of powerful spirits at our beck and call. All we need to do is have my friend here howl with all his might and they will assemble here before you can move an inch. Don't try my patience. Let us pass without further ado and you will be spared." The little ones laughed once again and moved to the edge of the branches above Uncle Rabbit and Sesimite.

"What do you know about this tree, you furry groundling?" The elder one's eyes narrowed. Slowly, he moved into a position where Uncle Rabbit thought this silvered-haired grump would fly down from his branch and attack him. Uncle Rabbit knew he had to stand his ground or else they could be further delayed.

"I know that this is one of the sacred trees of this isle. I know that it can impart great knowledge. I also know that it can cast spells and charms to confuse and harm those who do not respect this hallowed ground. There's one more thing I know. Our armies can be here in a flash. They will chop this tree down. We have no use for myth and legend."

"So, you DO know where you are. Then you should also now who we are. But just in case you and the dim whittled oaf don't know, let me inform you. Count us. How many do you see?" The silvered-haired one waited.

"I'm not sure. It's hard to tell with so many of you barely visible in the leaves," said Uncle Rabbit. The elder one laughed so loud that the tree shook.

"You are a simple rabbit, aren't you?" said the elder one. "There are far fewer than you think. In fact, there are only seven of us."

Sesimite growled, trying to let them now that he could take them all at once and very quickly too.

"Calm down, Sesimite," commanded the elder one. Sesimite stopped mid-growl.

"What?" This startled Uncle Rabbit and Sesimite. How did they know who Sesimite was? Why did they know? This turned things in a different direction.

"Yes, Uncle Rabbit, we know who you are. Don't you now that this tree, the Eo Mugna, has its guardians. You should have done some checking before you stopped here. We are the seven guardians of the Eo Mugna. We have powers beyond your comprehension. Not only will no harm come to this sacred yew, but we also have the authority to repel any who wish it harm or use its knowledge for nefarious purposes. So, Uncle Rabbit and Sesimite, state your purpose."

As the elder one spoke, the other six spirits assembled around him. Their mood was no longer playful. Arrayed together on the branch just above Uncle Rabbit's head, they suddenly were a threat. Even the air sparked with an ominous energy. Uncle Rabbit pulled on Sesimite's sleeve and whispered, "We need to get out of here. I don't like the tone of these creatures." Sesimite started to move away from the tree.

"Not so fast," came a voice from somewhere deep in the branches. A new entity emerged from a shadow just above the others. This spirit was larger than the others, but not as tall as a human. She was dressed all in green. Her skin too was green, as were her brilliant eyes. The only thing not green was her hair. It was shimmering gold. She floated down to the branch just above Uncle Rabbit's and Sesimite's heads where the seven guardians were assembled. They made room for her to stand in the middle of them.

Her voice was lyrical but firm. "My guardians have been polite enough. You have been asked your purpose, but you plan on trying to flee from us. That cannot happen until we know your purpose. However, if you wish to run, please go ahead. Try." They didn't. They were too terrified to move. "You want to believe you are clever enough to outwit us, but you're not as clever as you think. I will ask you one last time to state your purpose in being in these woods."

Sesimite turned towards Uncle Rabbit with eyes pleading for him to say something.

Uncle Rabbit took a step forward and explained. His explanation was a lie. He didn't realize the mistake he was making.

"We are on a mission from our mistress. She has charged us with finding an ancient amulet with which she can cure her dying daughter of a mysterious ailment. We believe this magical amulet lies within the confines of Clonfert Cathedral. Perhaps you know of it?" He asked his question a bit too casually.

The Green Maiden knew he was lying, but she played along because sooner or later, they would reveal their true purpose.

It was her turn to deceive Uncle Rabbit.

"Yes, Uncle Rabbit, I know of such a thing. In fact, I also possess a special object that will help you find it. I will entrust it to you on the condition that you return it to me, here, within three days hence, whether you find the amulet you seek or not. Should you fail to return it, I will dispatch harpies to find you and bring you back. You cannot hide from us. If we have to come and find you, I will cast a spell that will bind you beneath this tree until the end of days. Do you understand?"

Uncle Rabbit and Sesimite were trapped. They had no choice but to agree.

"We do, my lady and would very much appreciate your help." Uncle Rabbit had no intention of returning. He remained convinced that his and Sesimite's powers could overcome this maiden and her charges if needed.

"Very well." She faded back into the branches. She returned shortly with a crystal orb about this size of a duck's egg. On seeing it, Sesimite released a low moan as if he were falling into a swoon. The Green Maiden took notice. Uncle Rabbit reached up to accept it, but she gently pushed away his hand.

"Uncle Rabbit," she said, "you must not take this object for granted, nor think of it as a toy. This Druid's Glass is a wondrous and powerful object. It can repel all things sinister and harmful. I can lead you in the direction of your intentions. It can also toss you into danger and chaos, should you abuse it. Do you still want to accept it under the conditions I have imposed?"

Uncle Rabbit was giddy with anticipation. "Oh yes, dear lady. I am." He reached out his hand. The Green Maiden placed the Druid's Glass reverently on his upturned palm. She held his gaze as she folded his fingers over the orb and squeezed them together hard. Uncle Rabbit flinched from the pain of her grip.

The Green Maiden issued her warning again. "You will return three days hence or else." She dissolved back into the branches. The guardians likewise withdrew.

Uncle Rabbit motioned Sesimite to follow him. It was time to get away from the Eo Mugna Tree. Uncle Rabbit placed some distance between them and the tree with its spirits and the Green Maiden when he stopped. He pulled Sesimite into a cluster of bushes just in case they were being followed.

"This is a miracle, Sesimite. This orb, this Druid's Glass, will lead us right to the person in Clonfert House we need to find. What a fortunate set of circumstances!" Uncle Rabbit was so delighted that he hopped around joyfully in a circle until Sesimite reached down and grabbed him by the ears. As Sesimite held him dangling in the air, Sesimite transformed into a troll and spoke. It was the first time Uncle Rabbit ever heard Sesimite utter a word.

"I don't like this, Uncle Rabbit. Why would these creatures help us? And that lie you told about the general's daughter. What if she could tell you were lying?"

Uncle Rabbit squirmed out for Sesimite's grasp. "That's ridiculous. She is just a kind maiden helping out kindred spirits. Don't worry. Everything will be fine."

Sesimite wasn't so sure. "What if we can't find the student we are looking for, or, or, or if we get caught?" Sesimite asked, worried about the possible consequences.

"We will find this student. It's your job to make sure we don't get caught. Now let's get going."

Sesimite hesitated before he asked, "What if we can't in the three days she has given us? Then what will we do?"

Uncle Rabbit snorted, "We are never going to return this orb. It's ours now. Who knows, we might need it as a bargaining chip with Adena."

"But…" Sesimite started to say.

"No 'buts' Sesimite." With that, they fled towards Clonfert House.

What Uncle Rabbit and Sesimite didn't know was that the Green Maiden had a special relationship with Clonfert House. Her ancestors were among those creatures Saint Brendan had re-moved to the Land of the Saints all those centuries ago. Many eons later, with the help of those who were native to the Land of the Saints, her ancestors made their way back to the isle of their origins. They were met by the descendants of Mag Aedha, Scrivener, on the fateful voyage. Together, they were instrumental in assembling the thirteen families who would eventually enter into the Brendan Compact.

The Green Maiden gave Uncle Rabbit and Sesimite the Druid's Glass not to help them, but because, with it in their possession, she could follow their every move. When necessary, it would allow her to inform anyone in danger of their presence. Once Uncle Rabbit and Sesimite departed, she assembled the seven guardians in her lair high up in the Eo Mugna Tree. There, they sat around a magnificent crystal ball. Soon, Uncle Rabbit and Sesimite would appear in the crystal ball. The Green Maiden and the seven guardians would know all.

Chapter Nine

Galway, Ireland
Uncle Rabbit and Sesimite
Approach Clonfert House

Sesimite was the first to see Clonfert House because he had returned to his shape as a giant and could see above the dense brush. Both he and Uncle Rabbit would be able to see Clonfert House because, despite its invisibility to the human world, it was always visible to the spirit world. Sesimite let out a low, fierce growl.

"What is it, Sesimite?" Uncle Rabbit asked, hopping up and down and trying to see what Sesimite was looking at. He knew they were close to Clonfert House.

"Is it Clonfert House? Pick me up so I can see." Sesimite reached down and plucked Uncle Rabbit up by the ears. Uncle Rabbit hated to be picked up by the ears.

"Don't make this grabbing by the ears a habit or…" Uncle Rabbit stopped. There in the distance was Clonfert House.

"Put me down," he demanded. "We can't be seen. Who knows what those enchanters can do, even from a distance?

You should shift into a more benign form." Sesimite shape-shifted into a rabbit.

"Is this benign enough for you?" he said, taunting Uncle Rabbit. Uncle Rabbit was not amused but thought it was as good a disguise as any. It also allowed Sesimite to speak.

"Sesimite, let's stop for today. Let's try using the Druid's Glass to show us how to get into Clonfert House."

"Good idea, Uncle Rabbit," Sesimite said. "Let's go over there under those berry bushes. We should be safe there. Besides, I'm hungry." They hopped off to the shelter of the berry bushes.

Back at the Eo Mugna Tree, the Green Maiden and the seven guardians watched. When they witnessed Sesimite transform into a rabbit, when they heard what Uncle Rabbit said, they all were alarmed. One of the pixies spoke.

"They lied!" The other guardians joined a chorus of, "They lied. They lied!" The Green Maiden raised her left hand to silence them.

"Yes, they lied," she said knowingly.

"You knew," one of the guardians asked, surprised.

"I did," she replied. "I didn't know what their true purpose was, but I knew that what they told us about the mistress and the amulet was not true. If there was such an amulet, I would know of it. There isn't one like he described. It's because he lied that I gave them the Druid's Glass so that we could find out. Now we know that they have another purpose. We must do our best to discover what that purpose is."

"But how?" another guardian asked.

"We can only monitor them in the crystal ball for now. However, one of you, Botsam, it shall be you. Go immediately to Clonfert House. Inform the librarian, Professor O'Riley, what we know so far. Once we know more, another of you will be dispatched to update the professor. For now, we must be patient. Botsam, go to the librarian and share what we know. Insist that he set a watch. Don't forget to inform him that Sesimite is a shape-shifter and we may not know how he will present himself, though it will most likely be in the form of a rabbit."

Botsam vanished. Within an hour, he would arrive at Clonfert House. Meanwhile, all the Green Maiden and the other guardians could do was watch and listen to Uncle Rabbit and Sesimite.

*

Uncle Rabbit placed the Druid's Glass on the ground in front of him and Sesimite. They both stared at it, not sure what to do next.

Sesimite asked, "Why didn't you ask how to use this thing?"

"I thought it would be obvious once we got to use it. I think the Green Maiden said it would follow our intentions, so let's try that." Uncle Rabbit focused his attention on the orb while Sesimite watched.

"Sesimite," Uncle Rabbit whispered, afraid he might be heard, "you have to do this too."

Sesimite looked puzzled. "What am I supposed to do?"

"Keep thinking, 'How do we get into Clonfert House without being detected?' Just keep thinking that thought over and over. We will have to see what happens," Uncle Rabbit instructed Sesimite.

"Okay," Sesimite said. He too focused on the Druid's Glass while repeating, 'How do we get into Clonfert House?'

Up in the branches of the Eo Murga Tree, the Green Maiden and the six remaining guardians watched the crystal ball.

Several minutes passed before anything happened in either the Druid's Glass or the crystal ball. Then the Druid's Glass turned a milky white inside. Clouds swirled inside the orb. Uncle Rabbit and Sesimite were transfixed. The Green Maiden leaned in closer to the crystal ball. She saw exactly what Uncle Rabbit and Sesimite saw.

The swirling inside the Druid's Glass slowed to a stop. The clouds inside it drifted apart to reveal Clonfert House in its entirety. While all watched, the orb zoomed into a small corner of the foundation of one of the buildings. Zooming in further, a small breach was revealed just above the ground, a few feet from the corner of the building. It was just big enough for Uncle Rabbit and Sesimite, as a rabbit, to fit through. The only thing was that because they had never been to Clonfert House before, they didn't know which building it was. The Green Maiden didn't know which building it was either, even though she had been to Clonfert House many times.

Uncle Rabbit whispered again, "Sesimite, keep thinking, 'Which building is this? Which building is this?'" The two of them concentrated and watched the Druid's Glass closely.

Even though she wanted to know the answer, the Green Maiden knew it was better if Uncle Rabbit and Sesimite didn't and would have to explore to discover it. This would leave them out in the open and vulnerable. She instructed the guardians to match their intentions to hers so that they thought as one. Together, they kept repeating, 'Do not tell them. Do not tell them.' The Druid's Glass was pledged to the Green Maiden. It would give her intention precedence over that of Uncle Rabbit and Sesimite.

The Druid's Glass turned cloudy once again and then cleared to its natural clarity. It did not identify the specific building at Clonfert House that had the breach. Neither Uncle Rabbit and Sesimite nor the Green Maiden and the guardians knew where the entrance was located. But it was enough for the Green Maiden to send another guardian off to share what they knew so far with Professor O'Riley.

"Well, that's a start at least," Sesimite said.

Uncle Rabbit didn't share Sesimite's optimism. "Just how many buildings are there at Clonfert House? Where do we start looking? How do we keep from being discovered? This isn't as easy as I thought it would be." Uncle Rabbit was frustrated.

"Uncle Rabbit," Sesimite began, "we are just rabbits, as far as anyone would know. We can wander all over the place and not a single person will think anything of it."

"You are probably right," said Uncle Rabbit. "We will start off just before dawn in the morning. Hopefully, it won't take long." With that, they settled down to rest for the night.

The Green Maiden sent another guardian to tell the librarian to begin a search for any breaches in the walls of Clonfert House. Be on the lookout for two very busy rabbits working side by side. They would be Uncle Rabbit and the shape-shifter, Sesimite.

Chapter Ten

Galway, Ireland
Clonfert House
Professor O'Riley's
Office in the Library

Michael, Minda, Affey, and Kevin had been rushed into Professor O'Riley's office by Gianni Giannotti who announced to them while struggling for a breath, "Professor O'Riley needs you urgently in his office. Please, please no questions. We must hurry. Hurry." Not even Minda challenged Gianni. She remained silent. Now, sitting in O'Riley's office, she and probably the others were twitching with curiosity. Obviously, they were not going to be following the daily schedule this day.

Professor O'Riley burst through a door near the back of his office and went immediately to his desk.

"So glad to see the four of you. Pardon the urgency, but there have been some developments that require us to move with more haste than we had hoped." He spoke rapidly while sorting through some papers on his desk. "Ah, here it is." He stood up and read silently through two sheets of paper. He set them down on the desk. He looked at each of the four students sitting in front of him. He sighed heavily. He crossed to the table and sat in his oversized chair.

Minda couldn't resist any longer. "What is this all about, Professor. You're scaring my sister," she said and turned to check on Affey. Minda was scared too, but would never admit it.

"I'm fine, Minda," Affey said barely above a whisper.

"Minda, be patient, please. Things have evolved more quickly than we anticipated. We must make adjustments. I must ask each of you to forego your questions for now. There is work to be done and done quickly. I promise I will answer all your questions soon enough, but for now, please just listen and do as you are told."

Michael thought this would be very hard for Minda. He glanced at Kevin to see his reaction, but Kevin sat motionless, or maybe he was terrified. Michael couldn't tell which it was. Minda sighed and sat back against her chair, resigned, at least for the moment, to do as she was told.

Professor O'Riley continued, "There is much I want to tell you, but it must wait. Shortly, you will meet with your mentors. We had hoped your first meetings would be individually, but as circumstances have changed, you will meet together as a group—the four of you and your mentors. At that meeting, you will be assigned a task. We expect that the task will be undertaken immediately. We have no time to waste."

Minda leaned forward, poised to ask a question or maybe voice an objection. Professor O'Riley glared at her. She surrendered again.

"What I can tell you," Professor O'Riley began, "is that we have had several communications from our spirit-world colleagues that indicate there will be an attempt to penetrate the walls of Clonfert House in order to accomplish what we still don't know. We have a fairly good idea of where and how they will make their attempt, but not precisely when, though it seems imminent. Now, before you go to meet with your mentors, here are the discs Professor Chan Wu gave you. As you know, I had to modify them to make them useable for wider area than he set them. Here they are. Keep them safe. Only you four have one of these. The other students here don't even now they exist."

Michael, Minda, Affey, and Kevin each took one disc and placed them safely inside the pocket of their gray jacket. Just then, Gianni Giannotti crashed through the main door to the office. He was disheveled. He was having trouble catching his breath. Professor O'Riley jumped to his feet.

"Professor, you must hurry to the headmaster's office. I don't why. He just said to get you up there NOW!" Gianni fled back out through the doors. He wasn't wearing his signature lavender scarf.

"I must go. You four wait here. Someone will be with you shortly to escort you to your meeting with your mentors." Professor O'Riley moved swiftly to the door at the back of his office. He stopped before closing the door. "One more thing. You must look out for one another. This is very important for you to remember. You must stick together. Only use those discs if you find yourself alone and without any other recourse. We may not always be there to help you." He left.

The four of them sat silently. Each wondered which one of them was most afraid of what was happening. It took a few minutes before Affey spoke up.

"I trust each of you to watch out for me. I hope you all feel the same about one another. I think this is not going to end well." She lowered her head. Michael thought he heard her stifle a cry. Kevin moved a chair from the end of the table and sat close to Affey, who leaned over towards him.

"Oh, for goodness' sake, Affey. Do you have to be so melodramatic? Maybe this is all some sort of test for us." Minda was back to her old self.

Kevin had had enough of Minda.

"Oh shut up, Minda! Can't you see Affey is scared? She's your sister. Have some empathy." He reached over and took Affey's hand. She didn't resist.

"Let's all calm down," Michael said, trying to defuse the tension that was in the air. "Whatever they are going to ask us to do, we have to be at our best. We must do as Professor O'Riley asked. Be quiet. Do what we are asked to do. He asked us to look out for each other and we must."

Minda threw Michael a contemptuous look, but then something in the back of her mind suggested he was right. She looked him softly and said, "I'm sorry. I know I can be a...How can I say it politely...?"

Kevin was about to say the word when Gianni Giannotti burst in again.

"Alright, you four, follow me. Hurry. Hurry!" He flew out the door. They were swept along in his wake.

After swerving around more corners than they could count and going up and down a dizzying series of stairs, they arrived abruptly in front of a massive, vaulted set of steel doors. They had a patina from centuries of hands pushing their way in. There were no locks or latches, no hinges, and no knobs. Gianni almost crashed into the doors in his haste to get the four of them inside as soon as possible. He snapped around to face them. The look on his face was something between panic and responsibility.

"Wait here until these doors open and then hurry inside. You must hurry!" Then he was gone once again.

Chapter Eleven

Galway, Ireland
Clonfert House
Meeting the Mentors
Tasks Assigned

No sooner had Gianni disappeared than the doors creaked open. Stretching out before Michael, Minda, Affey, and Kevin was a cavernous, dimly lit room. The only light came from some torches in sconces along the walls and a few candelabras on the long wooden table that stretched towards the back of the room. They entered slowly, unsure of where to go or what to do. Then, they heard the creaking of more doors in the distant shadows of the room. Four separate doors opened and closed, each coming from a different direction. The click-clack of heels striking the stone floor grew louder and louder until, at last, they stopped. Four gray-robed figures were aligned along one side of the table. One of the four, a woman, motioned Michael, Kevin, Minda and Affey to sit opposite where the four figures were standing. Michael moved first, followed by Minda, then

Affey, and then Kevin. After they were seated, the four robed figures sat.

"We are professors. Smiley," she said, indicating herself, "Howenstein, Mbaye, and Caracova." Each nodded as they were introduced.

Professor Smiley, an American ancient beauty with long silver hair and blue eyes, continued.

"As Professor O'Riley has told you, there have been some unusual developments that require we adjust the timing of your training. We had wanted our first meetings with you to be individual, but alas! That is not possible."

Professor Mbaye, a striking, tall, ebony-skinned woman joined in, her accent pointed to Africa, perhaps Senegal. "Yes, we must accelerate things starting now."

"We know you have questions," said Professor Caracova, a squat woman of indeterminate age. She had a Slavic accent. "But they must wait." She directed her last comment to Minda specifically.

"Yes, questions, questions, questions," Professor Howenstein said as if his words were questions themselves. He had a severe countenance that matched the piercing tone of his voice. "Soooo many questions. Where shall we begin?"

Professor Smiley interrupted him, "Fritz, not now."

'What did that mean?' the four of the students each thought.

"Professor Mbaye, will you please outline generally what will happen next," Professor Smiley said.

"Yes, professor, I shall." Professor Mbaye leaned slightly forward, folded her hands on the table, and explained.

"We had, at first, hoped to assess the current level of your abilities. But events have overtaken our initial plans. We must prepare for an upcoming encounter that will enable us to observe your skills while at the same providing an initial defense of these walls."

On hearing the phrase 'in defense of these walls,' Affey let out a small gasp. It rattled Michael and Kevin. Minda reached under the table and pinched Affey's knee. The four professors took note of Affey's response.

Professor Mbaye made no mention of Affey's gasp as she continued her explanation.

"Each of you will be assigned a task. Each of those tasks relates to and affects the others' tasks. Each task must be completed perfectly or each of you will have failed. Failure puts Clonfert House at great risk." Minda pinched Affey again to make sure she didn't let out another gasp. "However, that does not mean you will be leaving here or your training will stop. It will just mean we will have to make more adjustments. Professor Howenstein, please continue." Professor Mbaye leaned back away from the table.

Professor Howenstein sat up rigidly. "We have learned that there is a weakness in the foundation of Saint Brendan's Cathedral. Specifically, there is a small breach in the foundation that we would like sealed." He didn't explain why. "However, the cathedral is visited daily by many pilgrims. While we would like to shut it down to seal the breach, it would raise too many questions. So, we have devised a plan that involves each of you employing the skill unique to you that will lead to the sealing of the breach." He handed the explanation off to Professor Caracova.

She began, "In a few minutes, each of you will accompany one of us to another chamber adjacent to this room. There, you will receive a sealed envelope. This is so only you, and of course each of us, know its contents. You may not under any circumstances reveal what your letter contains to any other person, nor is it permissible for you to address the contents with us. This is to ensure that there are no outside influences." Having finished, she and the other three professors stood up.

"Michael, you will come with me," said Professor Caracova.

"Affey, please come with me," said Professor Howenstein.

"Kevin, with me please," said Professor Smiley.

"Minda, follow me," said Professor Mbaye.

Each fell in line behind their assigned professor. Minda squeezed Affey's hand to reassure her. Affey ignored the touch.

Kevin looked towards Michael. They both shrugged.

Each of the professor-student pairs disappeared behind a door the others couldn't see.

Each of the students was ushered into a small room. Each room had a thick wooden table and equally thick chair, though only one. There was a single window of amber glass that let in light but obscured whatever might be seen outside. The walls were adorned with small tapestries depicting past encounters between the spirit world and the human world. Surprisingly, there were no books, manuscripts, or any instruments with which to write. There was a single door. It was as if the room was intended to block out the world and likewise foreclose any attempt to reach out to it from the confines of the chamber. Each of the rooms to which the four had been led was identical.

On each of the tables was a large envelope with the student's name handwritten in a formal script on it. Each envelope contained first a general statement of the circumstances of the task. Second were the specific instructions for the particular student. They opened their envelopes and trembled at the challenge they had each been given.

The general statement each received was this:

We, the magisterium, have been informed that there are two creatures from the western quarter that are about to arrive here. One comes in the form of a hare and is called Uncle Rabbit. The other is a notorious shape-shifter known for his cunningness. His name is Sesimite. While we know of their approach, we do not as yet know their purpose, though it no doubt is nefarious and must, of course, involve the sacred scrolls. Fortunately, the Green Maiden has deceived them by giving them a Druid's Glass. Unbeknownst to Uncle Rabbit and Sesimite, she sensed their rude intentions and placed the Druid's Glass with them so that she could monitor their movements, thus discovering their purpose of coming here. As of today, she has dispatched two guardians who have informed us that Uncle Rabbit and Sesimite are on the outskirts of Clonfert House. Sesimite has shifted into the form of a rabbit. They will be seeking entry via a small breach in the foundation of Saint Brendan's Cathedral. The magisterium has searched all the other buildings and found several other breaches. All have been sealed except the one in the foundation of Saint

Brendan's Cathedral. That breach was deliberately left open so that we can trap Uncle Rabbit and Sesimite once they enter. Each of you has been assigned a specific task based on the current state of your powers. The goal is to capture Uncle Rabbit and Sesimite. Your mentors will then take over and interrogate them so as to discover their purpose of being here. As you were told before entreating this room, you will have no contact with your fellow students. Yet, each of your individual tasks is working in concert with the others to affect the result we need. May fortune shine upon us all!

Michael had one thought after reading true general statement—this isn't going to work. He wasn't sure why; just an ominous feeling clouded over him.

Minda similarly had a sense of dread, but she quickly dismissed it because she was more interested in the contents of her second page.

Kevin had a surprising reaction. Usually being the cautious one, his feelings turned towards exhilaration.

Poor Affey sat alone in her room, a bit bewildered. She too often relied on Minda in situations like this. As she grew closer to Kevin, she missed his reassuring glances. Little did she know what was required ahead for her in particular.

While each of them read the elements of the tasks assigned to them, their respective mentors watched them from across the table. They were looking for any signs of weakness or hesitation, anything that indicated special care might be needed. Only Affey raised some concerns at first, but once she read her second page, an intensity rose in her that belied her initial fears.

Michael thought he probably had the most difficult task, though he couldn't possibly know for sure, since they had no contact with one another. The second page of the contents of the envelope explained that it was up to him to try to locate Uncle Rabbit and Sesimite before they entered the breach. He was instructed to change into ordinary clothes and wander outside the walls of the cathedral, posing as a visitor. It then described to specific steps he was to take.

After changing into normal clothes, he was to go first to the entrance of the cathedral and pick up a map of the gardens surrounding the cathedral. Then, he was to go to the information desk where he would be given an audio guide. He would be provided any new information via the audio device. He would also be monitored through the device so that whatever he found would be immediately known to the mentors. This was a ruse to make him look like the other pilgrims visiting the cathedral. In reality, the mentors wouldn't be monitoring him at all via the audio device. They had another more direct way of following his every move. It involved Minda. Most importantly, he was not to take any action against Uncle Rabbit or Sesimite whatsoever. His task was just to find them and observe their movements. The challenge for Michael was not being discovered by Uncle Rabbit or Sesimite. To help him with avoiding discovery, he was instructed to use his powers of thought-bending. More specifically, he was to find a balance between twisting Uncle Rabbit and Sesimite's thoughts away from identifying him as an observer while at the same time allowing them to think freely about what they were up to. Michael had never done this before. He wasn't sure how to accomplish this. So, he asked his professor, Caracova.

"I don't know how to do this. At least I've never done it before. I mean, thought-bending and not thought-bending. How do I...?"

The professor interrupted him, "Michael, you do know how. The fact that you haven't done it before doesn't means you cannot. When the time comes, you will know. Trust yourself. It may be a struggle at first, but it will come to you quickly once it is required of you." Michael didn't like the professor's words, but what choice did he have?

"Now off you go, Michael. Remember, first get the map and the audio device. We will be in constant contact with you, and if there is trouble, we will come to you." Professor Caracova opened the door where Gianni Giannotti stood, waiting to take Michael back to his room to change.

Minda was eager to get to her second page. When she read through it, she was both confused and thrilled. She read it a second and a third time.

"Professor Mbaye, do I understand this correctly? Am I really supposed to consciousness-mirror Michael? We've been taught not to use our powers on other enchanters."

Professor Mbaye's response was terse. "Just do as you are asked. We don't have time to explain right now." Minda was not to be cut off.

"I must know the reason for this. I'm not sure I can do what you've asked unless I know why." She started at Professor Mbaye, daring her not to explain.

With a huff, the professor said, "Michael is exposed and vulnerable more than the rest of you. We have provided safeguards, but they might fail us. Your consciousness-mirroring powers are prodigious and you know it. Let's see how well you can do."

That was enough to satisfy Minda. "Okay," she said. "Where do I go? Do you want me to follow him?"

"You will remain with me here in this room. You must do this from here."

Minda had never had to consciousness-mirror anyone without being near them so she could see them. Unlike Michael, she had no doubt she could do it and do it better than any of them expected. Neither they nor she would be disappointed.

Affey's challenge required more of her physically and emotionally than the others. It was also the one task that, should it fail, would put the entirety of Clonfert House at risk.

Saint Brendan's Cathedral was a place of pilgrimage. Hundreds of pilgrims arrived daily to visit Saint Brendan's tomb, see his relics, and enjoy the grounds. There was a slight chance that Uncle Rabbit and Sesimite might not try to enter until after the cathedral closed, but if they tried to enter during regular visiting hours, something had to be done to clear the cathedral without raising suspicions. They simply could not attempt to arrest Uncle Rabbit and Sesimite with pilgrims around.

Affey's most effective power was chaos-implementation. She could sow chaos subtly or profoundly. She had been called upon to do it more often than any of the others had been called upon to use theirs. Even her sister, Minda, had no idea. However, unlike the others, Affey suffered physically and emotionally after she created chaos. As her power grew, so did its impact on her. It was of special concern to the magisterium. Given what they were asking of her now, they feared for Affey's wellbeing. She would be closely watched.

Affey read her second page once. She looked up at Professor Howenstein and nodded her head. She knew instinctively she would remain where she was. Past experience taught her she could project chaos from afar. "Just tell me when," was all she said.

"Soon, Affey, very soon. Would you like something to eat or drink while we wait?" asked Professor Howenstein.

"I'm fine," she replied. Affey folded her hands on her lap, lowered her head, and waited.

Kevin's specialty was transcendental-movement. His was a rare power. He could set aside everything and enter into a meditative state. In that state, he could move objects and transport virtually anything he focused upon to anywhere he chose. In his experience with his power so far, there didn't seem to be a limit or boundary. While in the past he'd only had to focus on a single solid object, today he was being asked to do something new. Today, he was being called upon to move water. He was going to have to use his power to transport enough water from the river twelve miles to the north into the basement of the Saint Brendan's Cathedral and flood it. The water would trap Uncle Rabbit and Sesimite long enough for them to be arrested, or at the very least block their escape. Once they were securely bound and under the control of the magisterium, he was to return the water to the river. The danger for Kevin was that he had to wait until Affey had established some level of chaos and the pilgrims had moved out of the cathedral. If he moved too quickly, some visitors might still be in the basement and be caught in the flood. It was a matter of coordinating his action with Affey's chaos-implementation. Since he had no idea of when she would have done this, he had to rely on Professor Smiley to tell him.

"Professor Smiley, I've never done anything like this before. I'm afraid of this. There is so much that could go wrong."

"I will be here with you. I can guide you if necessary. Our hope is that we do not get involved with you. We don't want to be of any influence. But we will if absolutely necessary."

A knock at the door interrupted them. It was Gianni Giannotti.

"Here is a note from the headmaster." Gianni handed Professor Smiley a sealed note. The same note had been delivered to each of the professors. It read: *"Michael is now roaming the grounds. Minda has made a strong connection with Michael's consciousness and can follow him at will. Unexpectedly, she is also sharing his vision in real time, so we see what he sees. This is an unexpected aspect of her skill; one we have never known any enchanter to possess before. We are most fortunate. Make sure your students are in the best state possible. We are moving quickly."*

Chapter Twelve

The Western Quarter
The Troops' Training Field

General Ah Puch had called together all of his captains at the western training grounds to explain to them Adena's plans to retake the scrolls. He was not surprised to hear their objections.

"Sir, how do we know that this time will be different? How can I convince my troops to once again face the sacrifice of great losses?" one of the captains asked.

"All I'm saying right now is that we must prepare just in case we are ordered to advance. Adena has spies embedded in Clonfert House who are providing her with valuable intelligence. However, I and the other generals, Votan and Cabrakan, are holding back committing us to this fight unless we are assured of victory." General Ah Puch tried to ease his men's skepticism, but he wasn't sure he did.

Another captain spoke up.

"No disrespect to Adena or to you, sir, but her intelligence in the past has been anything but intelligent. Somehow, Clonfert House always knows our plans. They were waiting for us and we suffered defeat."

"I understand your concern, but trust me when I say we will not advance unless I and the other generals agree that the intelligence warrants our commitment to Adena."

General Ah Puch listened to the muffled voices of his men and women talking amongst themselves. He heard more than one voice objecting to what he told them. Then, the major in command of the special women's unit stepped forward. It was Major Lisset.

Major Lisset was the first female elf to be given her own command. When General Ah Puch first selected her for command, he assigned some his best soldiers to be assigned to her. It was a mix of male and female spirits. Eventually, she dismissed all the males and formed her all-female force.

He should have known that selecting Major Lisset for promotion came with risk. She was an extraordinary leader. Her performance on the battlefield was the stuff of legend. She was also strong-willed and confident in her abilities. In the many years she served under the general, she had never questioned him, but he knew one day she would. There would come a day when she might possibly replace him. When that day came, he hoped he would be able to turn over the command of his armies to her because she was the best suited to succeed him. He just didn't expect her to challenge him this soon.

"General Ah Puch, I speak for all the female spirits in my command. We have always been loyal to you. You have been a staunch supporter of ours and employed us in some of the most difficult and arduous missions, but this is different. To once again march ahead without at least some assurance of victory is folly. While you and the other two generals might conclude that sacrifices will no doubt have to be made, we women reserve the right to make our own determination."

Even though he had a deep respect for Major Lisset, General Ah Puch did not tolerate dissension. He allowed certain room to express concern and raise questions, but this was defiance of the generals. He had to put a halt to this now. If he didn't, he might lose control.

"You have said more than was prudent, Major Lisset. Loyalty means you follow your generals, period. To do otherwise risks not only your position but also your life. Do I make myself clear, major?" He had never spoken to her in such terms before. They had always had a proper and professional relationship.

The hush that fell over the troops was tense. No one turned to see what the major would do, but each one of the men and women on the field held their breath, waiting for her response. This was a test of leadership that might change the course of events. In the back of their minds, they all wondered what would happen if Adena got wind of what was happening. General Ah Puch harbored the same concern. Nevertheless, Major Lisset was not deterred.

She began respectfully enough. "General, sir. I am merely saying that as women, we should have the opportunity to evaluate the information you receive for ourselves. If you are confident in your appraisal, then why fear that we would reach a different conclusion? If the intelligence is sound, then we too would follow it. That seems fair to me." She had backed General Ah Puch into a corner. He knew it. He also knew that to push this confrontation further would not serve his purposes in preparing for Adena's order to advance. He had to respond in a way that appeased her while not appearing to have given in to her. All eyes were on General Ah Puch. They all knew that the major had cornered him.

"Very well then, Major Lisset," he began. "We will broaden the group that evaluates what Adena sends us." Then he thought of a way to signal that he was still in charge. "In addition to you, we will include all those who hold both the rank of major, or higher, and also hold a field command. I believe that would make the decision-making group under my Command Number Eighteen." He made sure he emphasized 'my command.'

"Fair enough, general. Thank you for taking my concerns into account." Major Lisset was intent on having the last word.

General Ah Puch signaled his sergeant to dismiss the troops. They returned to their training regimens, awaiting further word.

Meanwhile, General Ah Puch sent a messenger to Generals Votan and Cabrakan, outlining his decision with regard to Major Lisset, seeking their advice. He would later learn from the messenger that each of the other generals had encountered a similar level of resistance, though nothing like what General Ah Puch had experienced with Major Lisset. They followed his suggestion and expanded their own decision-making committees. However, the troops were not happy. Restless troops make for difficult battles. Some way or another, the three generals had to quash this restlessness soon.

Major Lisset led her legions back to the Doon Well where they always encamped under circumstances like these. There, they would wait for word from General Ah Puch.

The Doon Well flowed with magical waters only when women were present. The major had been brought by her mother as an infant and submerged into the well as a form of initiation into their clan. The major and her followers were the last of the line of female spirits who were both warriors and alchemists. Though the major and her followers were aligned with the western spirits, historically they shared much more in common belief and cause with the eastern tribes. The major shifted her allegiance to the west several centuries ago when the eastern tribes fell under the spell of an evil goblin. Once they cast the spell aside, they invited the major to return, but she refused, claiming neutrality at the time. Even though she didn't return to the east, she maintained an emissary who communicated regularly with the magisterium. She wanted to keep all of her options open. The magisterium, for their part, wanted her to return, as it was committed to the preservation of her lineage. Upon arrival at the Doon Well, the major assembled her captains. She shared with them the conclusions she reached during their march back to the Doon Well.

"Sisters, I have decided we will not participate in this foray against the east. We all know of our history with the east. We all know the miserable failure the west has suffered in their attempts to recover the scrolls in the past. As descendants of the writers of those scrolls, we are pledged to preserve and protect them. We must keep them from falling into the hands of anyone who would use them to do harm. For eons now, the eastern tribes have fulfilled this same duty. I see no reason why they cannot this time. Our emissary has recounted often enough just how committed the humans in Clonfert House are to their protection as well. If the eastern tribes and the inhabitants of Clonfert House have successfully repelled Adena and the western tribes before, they will do so again. So, we will remain here on our ancestral grounds."

The women under her command cheered. She raised her hand to silence them.

"My sisters, make no mistake. We may yet have to engage in this battle. But when and under what circumstances is yet to be known. We too must maintain our training regimen. We must be vigilant. We may yet be set upon by forces at work beyond our boundaries. I must now rest, as should you. Saint Bridget, protect us."

Chapter Thirteen

Galway, Ireland
Uncle Rabbit and Sesimite
Arrive At Clonfert House

"Sesimite, can you please tread a little softer? You're a rabbit now, not a plodding hulk," Uncle Rabbit admonished Sesimite.

"I'm doing my best," Sesimite said, slightly annoyed. "Maybe I should become a flea and hitch a ride between your ears."

"Shhh, Sesimite. We are getting close enough that our voices will carry."

Sesimite grunted.

Uncle Rabbit paused to peer into the Druid's Glass once again to see if it was more specific about the breach's exact location. Once again, it clearly displayed the breach but didn't give the slightest hint as to which building it was. As he looked a little closer, the image in the glass blurred and then cleared to reveal another slightly different breach.

"Sesimite, there are two breaches, not one." Sesimite leaned in, but he didn't care one way or the other. He was there to protect Uncle Rabbit.

What they didn't realize was that the Green Maiden had projected the idea of a second breach into the Druid's Glass as a ruse to confuse Uncle Rabbit and Sesimite. Hopefully, it would give Clonfert House more time to locate them.

"I don't know which one we should look for." Uncle Rabbit scanned in the direction of Clonfert House. He could see all the buildings except Saint Brendan's Cathedral which was located in the center of the academy, protected all round by the other buildings. This was a deliberate, calculated plan by the architects who designed the cathedral. It was designed for events such as those that unfolded with Uncle Rabbit and Sesimite.

"We have to decide as best we can where we are most likely to find Adena's spy. I don't know how best to do that. Do you have any ideas?" he asked Sesimite.

"Me? How would I know?"

"Sometimes you're useless, Sesimite." Uncle Rabbit wished he had someone else with him to help make the decision about what to do next.

Back at the Eo Mugna, the Green Maiden watched Uncle Rabbit and Sesimite in the crystal ball. When she heard mention of a spy at Clonfert House, she knew this was a serious development that needed to be brought to Professor O'Riley's attention without delay. The Green Maiden immediately dispatched a third guardian to Clonfert House. She felt an urge to go herself, but it would be better to wait for further intelligence from Uncle Rabbit and Sesimite. This was a truly unexpected development. The spy needed to be caught before they could pass on anything to Adena. It also posed a dilemma. Should they wait until Uncle Rabbit and Sesimite identified the spy, or should they capture them without waiting and hope for other ways to discover who the spy was?

Unaware that the Druid's Glass displayed their every move and listened to their every word, Uncle Rabbit looked once more toward Clonfert House. He made a decision. They would go first to the foundation of Saint Brendan's Cathedral to search for a breach. They should be able go unnoticed in the gardens, as rabbits were plentiful there. Pilgrims wandering all around would provide further distractions.

"Sesimite, we are heading to the cathedral. Let's hope there is a breach in its foundation to let us in." They hopped off towards the cathedral gardens.

This was exactly what the Green Maiden wanted to know. She dispatched a fifth guardian to Professor O'Riley to tell him the cathedral was where they were headed.

Professor O'Riley met with the headmaster to share the news from the Green Maiden. The presence of a spy for Adena in their midst was deeply troubling. Who knew what this spy had learned and what the spy had provided Adena? Never in the history of Clonfert House had there been a spy before. There were no procedures or protocols for such a development. The two of them decided to consult with the four students' mentors to devise a plan. They now knew why Uncle Rabbit and Sesimite were there. Professor O'Riley pointed out the conundrum of waiting for more information or capturing Uncle Rabbit and Sesimite. In the end, they decided to capture Uncle Rabbit and Sesimite. As for the spy, maybe Uncle Rabbit or Sesimite already knew who it was. They just hadn't said so yet.

Uncle Rabbit and Sesimite made their way through the portal into Clonfert House and on to the cathedral gardens. There, Sesimite foraged without a care. Uncle Rabbit munched a bit of this and that and slowly moved towards the foundation of the cathedral. He lost sight of Sesimite at one point but scurried around quickly and dragged him to the foundation. They slipped behind some rose bushes to once again consult the Druid's Glass. This time, Uncle Rabbit noticed that there was a stem of lavender just visible in the corner of the image in the glass.

"Sesimite, do you see lavender anywhere? We have to find this lavender plant," Uncle Rabbit said, pointing to the glass. Sesimite stood up on his hind legs and sniffed. He nodded toward a patch of purple near the far corner of the cathedral.

The Green Maiden also saw the lavender and the breach. This time, she sent word to Professor O'Riley telepathically. Hopefully, no other creature would intercept it. It was why she used the guardians before. She didn't want her thoughts to be intercepted. This time was different. Every second counted. Risks had to be taken.

No sooner had she sent off her thoughts than Professor O'Riley received them. He rushed from his office to the headmaster's study. He didn't dare risk sending a messenger or project his thoughts.

Michael was strolling through the garden with a small group of pilgrims. He stopped occasionally to examine a flower. Even so, he continually swept his eyes over the gardens looking for rabbits. He saw several, but each one was alone. He didn't see any that looked like they were working together. When he stood up from picking a pansy, he saw them. He wandered slowly in their direction. A group of pilgrims blocked his view for a moment. He feared Uncle Rabbit and Sesimite would disappear. They didn't. When the pilgrims passed, he watched the two of them move towards the foundation wall.

Back in her chamber, Minda had maintained her consciousness-mirroring of Michael without interruption. She continually described what she was seeing to Professor Mbaye who encouraged her efforts.

"Don't lose sight of them. I must go and inform the headmaster." Just as Professor Mbaye opened the door, the headmaster and Professor O'Riley arrived.

"Headmaster, I was just coming to see you."

"I know. I know," the headmaster said breathlessly. "They are going to enter through a breach in the foundation of the cathedral. Please, go and bring the others here. We must begin now. It's best we are all together."

Professor Mbaye ran out to do as the headmaster directed.

Even with the commotion of the arrival of the headmaster and Professor O'Riley, Minda didn't drop her focus with Michael for a second. Then something caught her by surprise.

"Oh no!" she exclaimed. "I think they saw Michael."

"Why do you say this, Minda?" asked the headmaster.

"Because Uncle Rabbit and Sesimite were right at the threshold of the beach when Uncle Rabbit suddenly turned and looked directly at Micheal. His eyes narrowed and his ears perked up."

Once they found the lavender bush that was revealed in the Druid's Glass, Uncle Rabbit stopped. He didn't want them to enter the breach if anyone was watching them. He stood up on his hind legs and took one last look around.

"Get Michael out of there. Tell him to go inside the cathedral and wait," the headmaster directed Minda to tell Michael.

"Headmaster, I don't think he actually recognized Michael. How could he? Besides, nothing registered in Michael's consciousness."

"Minda, do as I told you and tell him." The headmaster was angry with her.

Minda sharpened her concentration and sent the headmaster's directions to Michael.

"What?" Michael said aloud. "Minda? What are you doing? Are you inside my head?"

'I have to tell him,' she thought. 'Yes, Michael, I was directed to consciousness-mirror you by the headmaster. It was for your protection. I'm sorry I had no choice.'

'Okay,' he thought, knowing she would 'hear' him. He sent her another thought also. 'You owe me for this. I'll go back into the cathedral and wait by the baptistery to hear from you, or should I say until you think me through to what's next?'

She shared Michael's thoughts with the headmaster but left out the part about her owing him.

The others now were in the room with them. The headmaster rattled off his directions. They were going to capture Uncle Rabbit and Sesimite as soon as they entered the cathedral basement.

"Affey, start. We need the pilgrims out of the way. They must not draw Uncle Rabbit or Sesimite's attention. We have them where we want them. Kevin, settle into that corner and prepare to flood the basement. Once they are inside, we will use the river water to block their escape."

Affey became utterly still. The others weren't sure she was even breathing. The professors watched her carefully for any signs of upset behavior.

Kevin withdrew to a shadowy corner. He cast his power towards the river. He churned it up in anticipation of a swift transport to the cathedral cellar.

The headmaster asked Minda if there was anything new from Michael.

"No, sir, he is next to the baptistery. He did go and peek through the he door to the cellar. I suppose he wanted to see if there was a clear way down." What Minda didn't share was that Michael intended to go into the basement once he knew Uncle Rabbit and Sesimite were inside. Minda advised against it, but his mind was set. She admired his courage and decided to go along with him. It was as close to the action as she was going to get.

At the Eo Mugna, the Green Maiden was alarmed. She had lost contact with the Druid's Glass. It could only mean one thing. Uncle Rabbit and Sesimite had entered the cathedral cellar. A Druid's Glass was useless inside consecrated buildings. Saint Brendan's Cathedral was the holiest place. She had nothing more to offer the headmaster. She let him know.

Affey suddenly flinched. She shifted awkwardly in her chair. Professor Howenstein flew to her side. "What's the matter, Affey? What can we do to help?"

She opened her eyes. "Something is getting in my way. It's like something is repelling my every intention. I don't know what it is, but I can't do this from here. I need to go to the cathedral." She stood up and stepped towards the door.

"Wait!" the headmaster interjected. "This is terrible. I don't know if we have time to move you there. I think it's only a matter of minutes before those creatures make their way up from the cellar and into the cathedral. We can't attempt to capture them up there. It must be in the cellar." He turned to Affey and spoke to her softly, "Can you please try to do this quickly from there? Perhaps if we all stepped out of the room and it is just you inside?"

"I doubt it, headmaster. I am going to the cathedral." Affey was typically shy, but when circumstances required it, she could not be persuaded to do anything other than what she thought was right. This was one of those moments. She brushed past the headmaster and went out the door.

The headmaster didn't have a choice. He wouldn't stop her. Too much was at stake. He must trust her.

"We will all go with her," the headmaster said. "Minda, tell Michael to watch for us." With that, they all fled to the cathedral.

Uncle Rabbit and Sesimite had discovered the breach in the cathedral's foundation and crept through it and into the cellar. The cellar was enormous. Vaulted ceilings, stacks of crates, statues large and small, and linens littered about as far as they could see.

"Sesimite, do you see any stairs leading up from here?"

Sesimite briefly shifted back into his giant form, looked around, but didn't see any stairs. There was so much stored in the cellar that his vision was blocked in all directions. He shifted back into being a rabbit.

"Didn't see one. Check the Druid's Glass," Sesimite suggested.

Uncle Rabbit pulled out the Druid's Glass. It was different. It was no longer crystal-clear. It had turned black. It so frightened Uncle Rabbit that he dropped it and it shattered. The noise of the breaking glass echoed through the cellar.

"Oh no, someone will hear this and come down here and find us." Uncle Rabbit panicked. "We must leave quickly."

Sesimite blocked his way. Simultaneously, Sesimite shifted into his normal giant self. This presented a problem because, as a giant, Sesimite couldn't speak. He could only grunt and growl.

"What are you doing, you oaf? Get out of my way. I'm not going to be subject to these humans and their humiliations." He attempted to scurry between Sesimite's legs, but Sesimite grabbed him by the ears and gave him a shake. At that moment, the bells in the cathedral rang out.

"Maybe we're safe after all. The bells will cover the sound of the shattering glass." Sesimite set Uncle Rabbit down and shifted back into his rabbit form. They both stood as still as theirs nerves would allow, waiting for what they weren't quite sure.

Chapter Fourteen

Galway, Ireland
Clonfert House
Saint Brendan's Cathedral Cellar
The Capture of Uncle Rabbit and Sesimite

Up in the cathedral, Affey sat in one of the confessionals to set about sowing chaos. When she first settled into the dark confessional box, she did a quick test of her skill to make sure there was nothing blocking her. There didn't seem to be anything creating an obstacle. As she sat there preparing, she had decided that chaos was too strong for the circumstance. Instead, she decided to create a diversion that would lead the pilgrims outside. She knew that the garden contained a rare species of plant that bloomed only every fifty years or so. Since it was almost fifty years ago that it had bloomed, having it bloom a little early couldn't hurt. Suddenly, a cry came from outside the cathedral doors.

"It's blooming. Its blooming! It's a miracle! It's not even fifty years yet!" an elderly nun was shouting from the main entrance of the cathedral.

The pilgrims filed out behind her to witness the miracle.

The headmaster and the professors wanted to go too, but this was the only chance they had to capture Uncle Rabbit.

'Affey, that was brilliant.' O'Riley congratulated her by sending her his thoughts.

Kevin, who had accompanied them to the cathedral, placed himself in the north apse. It was the furthest point from the door to the cellar. He thought he would be undisturbed there.

The headmaster shouted, "Kevin, now!"

Kevin cast his enchantment over the river. The river churned. Springs below its riverbed gushed. Despite the energy flowing through the river, no one on or near the river knew anything was happening. From all appearances, the river was normal, but much of its waters were about to flood into Saint Brendan's Cathedral's cellar.

"What is that sound?" Uncle Rabbit whispered to Sesimite.

"Sounds like rushing water. A lot of it," said Sesimite.

"Where is it coming from? Sounds like its moving very fast. Can you tell where it's coming from?" Uncle Rabbit was frantic.

Sesimite jumped on top of a stack of crates. "It is coming in everywhere. If we don't get out of here, we're going to drown." He too panicked. Uncle Rabbit jumped up next to Sesimite to see for himself.

"It's rising too fast. We will have to stay up here and hope it stops before it reaches us. I'm afraid we're trapped up here. Why is this happening?"

While Uncle Rabbit and Sesimite held on to each other atop the crates, Michael, despite having been told to stay where he was up in the cathedral, made his way down the stairs into the cellar. The water was rising fast. The bottom three steps were already under water. He was desperate to find Uncle Rabbit and Sesimite.

Minda lost contact with him. "Professors," she said, "Michael has started down into the cellar. For whatever reason, I have lost contact with him." For the first time, she was scared.

This was not a good idea. The professors looked at one another and without saying a word, they ran as one towards the cellar door. Kevin remained where he was in complete control of the incoming water.

What they all forgot was that Affey was still in the confessional, alone.

Despite her concentration, Affey began to feel unsettled. She heard commotion outside the confessional, which was the professors and Minda fleeing to the cellar. She was alone in the dark confessional and everything had gone quiet. She started to breathe quick, shallow breaths, a sure sign her anxiety was intensifying. When see peeked through the curtain on the confessional door, she realized she was alone. No one was in the cathedral. This was too much for her. She ran from the confessional into the center of the cathedral. She spun around looking for any place of safety. She didn't see one. 'The pilgrims must be in the garden. I'll go there and stay with them until Minda comes to find me. I must control myself or the enchantment of the pilgrims will end and then what will happen?' Affey walked quickly into the garden, struggling to remain calm so as not to lose her concentration on the enchantment she had cast over the pilgrims. When she reached the garden where the plant was blooming, she joined the rear of a group of pilgrims admiring the rare blooming plant. She struggled to maintain the enchantment, but it held.

Affey wasn't sure how much time had passed. It was near closing time and the pilgrims started to move to the exit of the cathedral gardens. Still alone and not knowing what else to do, she followed them out through the walls into the adjoining alleys. As the pilgrims dispersed, Affey was now utterly alone. Her breath was coming quicker and quicker. If she didn't find some help soon, she feared she might pass out. Unsure about whether to maintain the enchantment or not, she decided she no longer had the strength to hold it. She released the enchantment just as the sun slipped below the forest to the west. This helped return her breath to normal and she calmed down slightly. She was still terrified of being alone. She thought her only option was to make her way back towards the cathedral. She had only taken a few steps when a small creature blocked her way. It was one of the Green Maiden's guardians.

"Don't be afraid, Affey. I've been keeping watch over you. Your sister and the others are very busy at the moment. Events of great importance are unfolding. Unfortunately, they have forgotten about you for the moment. Returning to the cathedral alone is not safe. I am taking you to my mistress, the Green Maiden of the Eo Mugna. She will keep you safe and return you here soon."

Affey fainted. The guardian swept her up and transported her to the Green Maiden.

Back in the cellar, Michael saw Uncle Rabbit and Sesimite on top of the crates. They didn't see him. Moving as quietly as he could through the rising water, he approached them. Minda and the professors crept down the stairs. Now the bottom four steps were underwater. No one spoke. Minda caught sight of Michael and indicated his location to the others. Then she saw Uncle Rabbit and Sesimite. Michael was coming up behind the stack of crates Uncle Rabbit and Sesimite were standing on when he saw Minda approaching. She held a finger up to her mouth to tell him to be quiet. At this point, the headmaster had to intervene. He let loose a charm that suspended Michael and Minda in place. A second charm was released to bind Uncle Rabbit and Sesimite as well. The charm worked on Uncle Rabbit, but not Sesimite. Sesimite sensed something was wrong before the charm engulfed him. He had shape-shifted into the form of a fly and buzzed up into the rafters of the ceiling. From his position above them, he saw everything. He also saw the exact moment Uncle Rabbit fell under the charm's spell. Sesimite knew he couldn't do anything to help. He stayed just long enough to witness what happened to Uncle Rabbit. There was a small crack in the ceiling just above him. He took flight and escaped through it. As he flew into the fresh air, he knew he must inform Adena. This could mean the end of him. She didn't know he had been sent here. He would be tortured to explain things to her. Her rage would be boundless. Maybe it would be better to go to General Ah Puch and the other generals first. Hopefully, they could figure out some way to redeem the situation. If not, they were all doomed.

Chapter Fifteen

Galway, Ireland
Clonfert House
Uncle Rabbit Interrogated

Having found some chains in the cellar, the headmaster bound Uncle Rabbit so he couldn't flee. The spell the headmaster had cast to first subdue Uncle Rabbit had to be released if they were going to interrogate him. Minda and Michael were released from the charms that suspended them. Kevin had returned the waters to the river and joined them in the cellar. When Minda woke up from the spell, she looked around for Affey.

"Where's Affey?" she asked anxiously.

"She's right over…" Professor Howenstein started to say.

"Where is she?" Minda shouted.

"She's not here," Michael said. "I don't see her."

"Affey. Affey," they all called out for her. There was no response.

She needed to be found. Her absence was troubling. "Minda and Michael, go upstairs and find her. Bring her back down here to be with us," the headmaster ordered.

Minda and Michael quickly disappeared up the stairs into the cathedral. They searched the cathedral, the gardens, and surrounding forest to no avail. They even ran back through the halls of Clonfert House itself. They alerted Gianni Giannotti that Affey had gone missing. Gianni sounded the alarm throughout Clonfert House. This caused a great commotion. Students searched everywhere for her. Again, it was to no avail. All this commotion caught the attention of one particular student, a woman who had always kept to herself.

"What's going on?" she asked another student who was rushing by.

"One of the young students who arrived yesterday has gone missing. The headmaster is making a big deal about finding her." He continued on calling out Affey's name.

The woman wondered, 'Why would the headmaster be turning Clonfert House upside down to find this child? She probably just wandered off and will be back soon. Or there is something special about this girl. Come to think of it, why are these four teenagers here in the first place? I need to find out more.'

This particular student, Pyx by name, had been groomed by Adena for precisely this moment, though Pyx didn't know it. Adena had imparted the power to remote-view events taking place. Pyx pulled a mat from under her bed and sat crossed-legged on it. Closing her eyes and breathing deeply, she slowly panned over the entirety of Clonfert House. Other than the flurry of the search for Affey, nothing unusual was seen. Then she turned her attention to the cathedral.

As her vision threaded through the cathedral, she saw nothing at first. Then she noticed an open door to a staircase that led down below. She followed the stairs to see where they led. When she reached the bottom of the stairs, she saw the headmaster, the professors, Michael, Minda, and Kevin in a circle. They were all focused on whatever was inside the circle. She forced her view above them. There, struggling against the chains that bound him, was Uncle Rabbit.

'What is he doing here?' She was familiar with all of Adena's subjects, so she knew who Uncle Rabbit was. She thought it peculiar that he was here. He was no more than a clown, an annoyance. This had to be important. Why was he bound? He was harmless enough. She realized there was more at work here involving these scholars and children. 'I must report this to Jerome. He must pass this on to Adena.'

She pulled her vision back from the cellar. She got up from her mat. She summoned a sprite who could wing its way to Jerome's realm in an instant. She told the sprite to go to Jerome immediately and relate to him all that she saw. She made the sprite repeat every detail before she let it fly off. Once the sprite was gone, she packed her belongings. Later, under the cover of darkness, she would be gone. Her hope was that in the general confusion surrounding Affey, her own absence would go unnoticed. It was a small risk she had to take compared to the risk of being discovered as a spy for Adena. If Uncle Rabbit had been sent here, then Adena must be behind it. If she didn't report what she knew to Adena, then when Adena found out, it would only mean one thing: torture for her. She could not endure it. She had already taken care of that by dispatching the sprite to

Jerome with the information. If the headmaster found out why she was here, it would be over for her. She had to leave. Where to go was the question. Staying at Clonfert House was not an option. Adena's realm was not an option either, since she couldn't predict what Adena's reaction to all of this would be. She had to simply disappear.

Just before dawn, Pyx went down through the main hall towards the exit near the Sacred Well. Guards! She snuck around to the back entrance only to find more guards. These were the only two ways out and they were effectively sealed. The magisterium knew something. No one was getting in or out. Pyx had no choice but to return to her room and await her fate.

Meanwhile, Uncle Rabbit was moved to the Pillory by the Weeping Cross. The headmaster thought it the best place to extract information from Uncle Rabbit. The Weeping Cross was where one came to seek forgiveness and confess their transgressions. The Pillory was intended as merely a symbol of what the penitent would suffer if they didn't. It had been used only once in Clonfert House's history. Who it was and why was it shrouded in mystery?

"Oh no," Uncle Rabbit said, trying to push away from the Pillory. "You wouldn't dare do that to me." Uncle Rabbit had seen a Pillory used in Adena's camp. The one time he witnessed it being used, the poor fellow had his hands chopped off.

The headmaster said, "We won't unless you are uncooperative. We will use it if we have to."

"I have nothing to say," Uncle Rabbit said defiantly. Yet, he couldn't keep his ears from twitching, a sign of his fear.

Professor Smiley stepped forward. She spoke calmly and without urgency. "First, please tell us where your companion is hiding."

Uncle Rabbit laughed. "Hiding? He's gone. He's a shape-shifter. He's gone." He laughed again a little louder. In fact, Uncle Rabbit was bluffing. He didn't even know Sesimite was missing. His protector had abandoned him. His ears twitched again.

They all looked at one another. Minda spoke to no one in particular.

"Well, I'm sure he's off to tell whoever sent him here of what happened. I assume that's not a good thing."

"No, it is not, Minda," the headmaster said. "And please, you may stay and observe this. However, should you or Michael or Kevin utter another word, you will be sent back to your rooms. Understood?"

She stepped back between Michael and Kevin. They remained silent.

Professor Caracova was next. "Let's cut the heart of the matter. Why are you here?" They all knew he was here looking to make contact with a spy. What they were unsure of was if Uncle Rabbit knew who it was.

Uncle Rabbit glared at her.

The professor hardened her tone. "You WILL tell us. If you think you can remain uncooperative, we will use the Pillory to its full effect. So, I will ask you again. Why are you here?"

At this point, the headmaster took over. "I'm going to have to ask all of you to leave. I need a few minutes alone with Uncle Rabbit. That is your name, is it not?" he asked, facing Uncle Rabbit.

This shocked Uncle Rabbit. "How do you know who I am?"

The others, who had not yet left, were equally shocked.

"Yes, headmaster, how do you know?" asked Professor Smiley.

"As a headmaster, there is much I must now. This creature here is a subject of Adena."

The professors gasped. Minda, Michael, and Kevin had no idea what he was taking about, though before long they would.

"Now please, take your leave. Wait over there." The headmaster pointed towards a spot at the edge of the forest far enough away from the Weeping Cross and Pillory so that they could not hear what he would say to Uncle Rabbit. "I will call out to you when you can return."

They did as the headmaster told them. Once they were beyond earshot, the headmaster stepped in very close to Uncle Rabbit. He bent over until Uncle Rabbit could no longer avert his eyes from the headmaster's. The headmaster's eyes were fierce. They flashed with anger. Uncle Rabbit felt a threat coming from the headmaster, a threat beyond the pain of the Pillory.

"You listen to me. You will tell me everything you know or even think you might know. Guesses even. If you don't, I won't use the pillory. There is something much, much more painful for you. You see, I have a colleague on her way here. She will arrive momentarily. Once she does, you will have one single opportunity to answer me. If you do not, she will take you away forever."

Uncle Rabbit had never seen such intensity in another creature of any kind. Even though he knew that the headmaster meant every word he said, Uncle Rabbit could not and would not betray his friends. He stared back at the headmaster.

"I shall tell you nothing. Besides, there is nothing I know," he lied.

Just then, Uncle Rabbit heard a whoosh in the forest. He blinked his eyes once and there before him stood the Green Maiden. He never thought he would see her again. But seeing her now, under these circumstances, was at once terrifying and beguiling. She was accompanied by Affey. The headmaster had no idea that Affey was with the Green Maiden or why. This was not the time to inquire. He was certain the Green Maiden would explain soon enough.

From where they stood waiting to be recalled by the headmaster, Minda was the first to see Affey. She was about to call out her name when Professor Mbaye clasped her hand over her mouth.

"You must remain quiet. Affey is safe. She is with the Green Maiden. I will tell you about the Green Maiden later. Affey will explain why she is with her. We must be patient."

Minda nodded. Professor Mbaye removed her hand from Minda's mouth.

"Uncle Rabbit," the headmaster said, turning Uncle Rabbit's face towards him. "This is your last chance. I mean it. Your last chance." He paused in order to give Uncle Rabbit an extra moment to reconsider. "Who is the spy your mistress has placed in our midst?"

Shocked yet again by the headmaster's knowledge, Uncle Rabbit, resigned to his fate, said, "Don't know who the spy is." At least the headmaster confirmed the fact that there was a spy. Uncle Rabbit knew they would never believe him, but he hoped that maybe they would. He looked imploringly first to the headmaster and then to the Green Maiden. "I don't know."

Uncle Rabbit had lied too often. They simply didn't believe him anymore.

"Enough!" The headmaster was finished with Uncle Rabbit. He said to the Green Maiden, "Take him, madam. He is no longer of use to anyone in this or any other world." He then spoke one last time to Uncle Rabbit. "We shall not meet again. Nor, I'm afraid, shall you see Adena again, which perhaps is best for you." He signaled the Green Maiden to take Uncle Rabbit away. The two of them dissolved into thin air and were gone.

The Green Maiden took Uncle Rabbit to the Eo Mugna. Just as she had threatened him when she gave him the Druid's Glass, she bound him down among the great roots of the tree. The roots wound him round and round. He sank ever so slowly below the earth. He remained there until the end of time, bound and twisted among the roots of the Eo Mugna. In time, even the memory of him would be erased.

While the headmaster and the Green Maiden dealt with Uncle Rabbit, Affey was taken into the arms of her sister. At last, she was safe. Much later, she would tell them what she saw while she was with the Green Maiden. For now, though, being with her sister and friends was enough.

The headmaster signaled the professors and the students to return to the Pillory and the Weeping Cross.

"I know all of you have questions. Not now though. Uncle Rabbit remained uncooperative and the Green Maiden will deal with him. Let us return to Clonfert House. Before we do, I must share something with you. All that has happened, all that you have witnessed today must remain with us alone. Adena, whom your four young ones don't know, but will soon, has placed a spy among us. Discovering the identity of this spy is of urgent concern. Professors, please return and call a general assembly for tomorrow morning. You four are to remain in your rooms until called for. You may stay together if you wish, but you must not under any circumstances leave the floor of your building. Is that clear?" Each of them nodded 'yes' in return.

"Very well. It's late and we are all tired and hungry." He gestured that the students should lead them back to Clonfert House. When they reached the entrance to the student's building, he spoke to them again.

"These are very dangerous times. You four were brought here to join the defense of this institution and all it holds. We had hoped there would be more time to prepare you, but events of the past few days have changed that. We will make adjustments. Have no fear. You will be prepared. We will once again prevail. Now, get something to eat and rest. Take special care of Affey. She looks exhausted." The headmaster and the other professors left. Kevin and Minda helped Affey up to her room. Michael watched as the headmaster and the professors disappeared around a corner.

He spoke his thoughts aloud quietly because he wanted to hear his own words. "I want to go home. I don't like any of this anymore. I wonder what my aunt would tell me to do if she were here. And poor Uncle Rabbit! What is his fate? I guess I should ask that about all of us. What is our fate?"

Chapter Sixteen

In the Western Quarter
Adena's Rage

The sprite related everything that happened at Clonfert House to Jerome. Knowing the urgency of the news and the risk to himself in delaying notifying Adena, he wasted no time in sending a message to her that he had news. The time Adena had given was almost up, so the arrival of the sprite could not have been more auspicious. He paced for hours, waiting for Adena to arrive. He hoped he would not bear the brunt of her anger.

"Jerome," a voice called from outside his door. "You are summoned."

Adena had arrived. As he walked to Adena's throne room, he considered how to deliver his news. She would not take it very well. It would be best just to tell her what he knew without any hesitation. It was dawn. The sun was rising behind him as he entered the throne room. He could make out the outline of her two attendant manticores. Her throne was deep in shadow and he didn't know if she sat there or not.

"Jerome, you have news for me. I trust it is good news. I'm in no mood for anything else." Adena's voice carried a threat. Jerome cleared his throat. She gestured for him to take a seat on the stool that was on the floor in front of her throne.

"Forgive me, mistress, but what news I have is deeply disturbing. I would be remiss in not telling it to you without hesitation. I beg you not to place the blame for this news upon me. I only can tell you what I have been told."

Her patience was already at an end. "For goodness' sake, Jerome. Out with it." She stood up to signal her growing anger.

"Uncle Rabbit was caught in the cellar of the Saint Brendan's Cathedral at Clonfert House. He has been bound by the headmaster and taken to the Pillory at the Weeping Cross. Your spy among the students at Clonfert House, Mistress Pyx, has seen all of this. Her messenger brought me this news just this night. I did not delay in calling for you."

"Uncle Rabbit!" Adena said, spitting his name through her teeth. "What was he doing there?" She paused for a second to think. "Someone has deceived me. Someone sent Uncle Rabbit to Clonfert House. Why? I will know who it is. They will feel the full fury of my wrath. Jerome, you have done well enough. I will spare you this time. Send your sprite back to Pyx. She is to be told that she needs to get to Uncle Rabbit and rescue him. He is to be brought without delay to me." Adena didn't wait for Jerome to respond. She exited the throne room, her robes fluttering behind her. Her manticores hissed and scurried off with her.

Adena left the realm where Jerome was held and went directly to the cave of the Dar Lantern. She posted her manticores at its entrance so she could consult the oracle who dwelled in the cave's depths. The Oracle of the Dar Lantern was consulted by creatures of the spirit realm in times of great difficulty or when momentous decisions were to be made. The Oracle, being neither male nor female, neither spirit nor human, held no allegiance to either. The Oracle's only loyalty was to the truth of the visions that came into view. It was this independence that made the Oracle renowned. The Oracle of the Dar Lantern was also always right in the predictions that came from the Dar Lantern.

The Dar Lantern was held in a secret chamber somewhere inside the Oracle's cave. Only the Oracle could see it or use it. Adena had once thought of imprisoning the Oracle's predecessor, but under threat of a terrible curse, she abandoned her plans. Still, the Oracle of the Dar Lantern was skeptical about Adena's arrival.

Even before she arrived at the Cave of the Dar Lantern, Adena heard the Oracle's voice.

"Adena, you are angry. There is more anger than I have seen in you before." The Oracle's voice was pure, nurturing, and musical.

Adena approached the steps of the Cave of the Dar Lantern and said, "Anger doesn't begin to describe what is welling up inside me. Someone has betrayed me." Her last comment, though angry, had a hint of sadness.

"Ah, betrayal," said the Oracle. The Oracle of the Dar Lantern stepped out of the cave's entrance to the top of the ramp, leading from where Adena stood to the cave's entrance. The Oracle always wore white. "Yes. What an awful thing is betrayal. It has brought ruin upon queens and kings for all of history. Even saints have been betrayed. It is a price the powerful someday must pay. This is a universal truth for all creatures of all realms."

"I don't need a lecture." Adena was overstepping the boundaries of decorum when speaking with the Oracle. "What I need is for you to tell me who the traitor is. I have no time for chitchat." She thought about taking a step up the ramp towards the Oracle but changed her mind when the Oracle began examining Adena from head to toe. Even though she didn't make a move towards the Oracle, Adena remained steely and fixed where she stood.

"This anger of yours obscures your thinking. First set it aside. Only then will I tell you what I know."

"I cannot and will not," Adena declared.

"Very well," said the Oracle. "Then what I can tell you will be obscured as well. Your rage is so radiant that it disrupts my visions."

"Just tell me what you know!" Adena screamed. She was losing control.

The Oracle cared not for the tribulations of those who sought advice. The Oracle resigned long ago to the vagaries of spirit and human emotion. All the Oracle could do was share the knowledge. Consequences were of no concern to the Oracle, nor was the Oracle willing to tolerate outbursts like Adena's.

"Please, Adena, join me inside. I will tell you all I know no matter the fact that your rage will blur what I see."

Adena followed the Oracle into the Room of Rituals. Adena had been in this room before. It was where the

Oracle's predecessor had threatened the curse. The Oracle sat before the altar facing Adena, who remained standing.

"Sit," the Oracle ordered. Adena sat down.

The Oracle's eyes closed. Several candles on the altar simultaneously lit up. A sweet-smelling fragrance filled the air. The Oracle's eyes opened. The Oracle said, "More than one has betrayed you. Try as I might, your anger disrupts my ability to see who they are. They are close to you. You have confided in them throughout your reign. For a reason I cannot fathom, they have lost confidence in you. One or more of them thinks your judgment is clouded. With regard to what I do not know."

Adena interrupted, "Are they female or male?"

"They are both," said the Oracle.

This confused Adena. Her closest confidants were men. There were few females whom she trusted because a female was far more able to spot her weaknesses than a male. She saw all females as a threat to her position.

The Oracle was watching Adena carefully for some clue as to why she might have been betrayed. Then, the Dar Lantern sent the Oracle a vision that was not affected by Adena's rage. The vision was of the sacred scrolls at Clonfert House.

"You are going after the scrolls again, aren't you?" This surprised the Oracle. The Oracle thought Adena's prior failures had taught her a lesson. Apparently, they only emboldened her.

"Yes, I am." Adena stood up. She had enough of the Oracle. She was leaving. The Oracle had nothing more to offer her.

"Adena, wait." The Oracle closed her eyes again. The Oracle was seeing something more. The Oracle's eyes opened wide. The Oracle would not tell Adena what the vision revealed. Adena could not be persuaded to abandon her plan to steal the scrolls anyway. All the Oracle said was, "This is folly, Adena. It might well be the end of you."

Adena fought to control her rage. "I will recover them this time. I had them once and I shall have them again. You will see."

Adena ran down the ramp and vanished into the air. The Oracle sat for a long while looking into the future. What she saw for Adena was bleak.

Once back in her own territory in the west, Adena dismissed the manticores, doubled the guard, and thought and thought about who had betrayed her. Was it General Ah Puch? Voltan? Cabrakan? No, they had been loyal to her always. Yes, they had concerns about another foray to steal the scrolls, but she knew they would not abandon her. Who was Uncle Rabbit familiar with besides them? The three generals knew him, but who else? She didn't know much about Uncle Rabbit at all. She just knew his reputation for conniving. She knew too that he could be bought for the right price. She had to find more about him before he was brought back to be questioned by her. Unfortunately for her, Uncle Rabbit was never coming back.

"Guard," she called out, "go and fetch me Master Foote."

Several minutes later, a small voice said through the curtain covering the entrance to her quarters, "It's Master Foote, mistress."

"You may enter, Master Foote."

Master Foote was an ancient bog fairy. Over the centuries, he had developed a wide network of informants. He was a walking library of information both useful and not so much. It was said that there wasn't a single spirit or human in the west that he didn't know. Others claimed this old bog fairy had lived too long and that his memories were twisted in knots. Adena didn't care. If Master Foote had information about Uncle Rabbit, she wanted to know about it. He shuffled into the room. Adena indicated he should take a seat at the table. She sat opposite him.

"To the point, Master Foote," Adena said. "Who is Uncle Rabbit and who employs him?"

"Hmmm..." said Master Foote. "Uncle Rabbit, Uncle Rabbit? Let me see..."

"Come on, Master Foote. Don't play games with me. You know who he is."

"I do, Mistress Adena. I'm trying to figure out how to say what I know. He's a slippery one. Last I knew, he was a compatriot with one Sesimite, a shape-shifter. You could employ them both for a price. In the past, this Uncle Rabbit could be counted on to hold his tongue. Very loyal they say if the price is right."

"And this Sesimite?" asked Adena.

"He's a bit of an enigma that one. Drifts in and out of my purview. Don't know much else about him."

"Let me ask you this, Master Foote. If I wanted to hire someone to betray a trust, would I approach either one of these two?"

"Oh yes, madam, especially Uncle Rabbit. Pay him well and he will hold his tongue. I'm sure there are limits to his loyalty, but barring a threat to his life, I wager he would be a grand choice."

"I have one last question for you, Master Foote. Do you have any knowledge that anyone close to me questions my leadership?"

Master Foote didn't want to answer this question. He was sure it was a trap that would not end well for him.

"Madam, all leaders have subjects who question them. All leaders are doubted from time to time. Not a single powerful leader has not suffered the whispers and rumors among those whom they lead."

"That's a clever response, Master Foote, but that doesn't answer my question."

"If it were me, mistress, if I truly believed someone had betrayed me, I would start with those most in a position to harm me."

"Thank you, Master Foote. That is all."

Master Foote shuffled out into the night. From his past experiences in matters such as these, he believed that things were going to take a nasty turn. It was best for him to depart for the hills.

If Master Foote was right about the possibility of those who could do her harm, it led to only one conclusion. Her deceiver was either General Ah Puch, Voltan, Cabrakan, or maybe all three.

Her rage swelled.

"Guard, send messengers to Generals Ah Puch, Voltan, and Cabrakan. They are to appear before me the day after tomorrow."

Whichever one of them it turned out to be, they would be made an example of. All would see the terrible consequences of betraying her.

Chapter Seventeen

In the Western Quarter
Sesimite Briefs the Generals

Sesimite went to General Ah Puch's camp first. He immediately shape-shifted to appear as one the general's guards so he could pass through the camp without being questioned. It also would allow him to speak. It was midday. Troops trained everywhere he looked. Clearly, they were getting onto a war footing. At General Ah Puch's tent, Sesimite was briefly detained by one of the guards, but after insisting he had urgent word for the general, he was admitted.

"General Ah Puch, it's me, Sesimite. I have taken on this form so that I can speak to you. I must inform you of what has befallen Uncle Rabbit."

General Ah Puch looked up from the table where he was examining several charts. "What did you say?"

"Sir, it is me, Sesimite, in the guise of one of your guards. I have bad news to convey."

General Ah Puch crossed from behind the table to inspect Sesimite. "If you are Sesimite, then briefly shift into another guise."

Sesimite shifted to his normal giant appearance and then shifted back quickly to the shape of a guard. This satisfied the general.

"Where is Uncle Rabbit?" General Ah Puch demanded, alarmed.

"I am afraid that I don't know. He was captured by the headmaster of Clonfert House and several professors. They bound him tight with chains. I shifted to become a fly so that I could go undetected. I stayed long enough to see them haul him off to what the headmaster said was the Pillory by the Weeping Cross. I was afraid they might discover me, so I fled and came directly here."

"You did the right thing, Sesimite, but this is bad news indeed. Very bad news. I suppose you didn't learn anything about the spy Adena placed inside Clonfert House?"

"No, sir, we did not," Sesimite said apologetically.

"Anything else you noticed that we should be worried about?"

"There was something unusual I thought," Sesimite said, but then said, "Maybe it's not important."

"What is it, Sesimite? Why are you hesitating?"

"Like I said, maybe it's nothing. It just seemed odd to me." Sesimite was looking for some encouragement from the general to speak. Sesimite was unsure how all of this was going to affect him. General Ah Puch didn't say a word.

"Well, sir, when the headmaster and the other professors captured Uncle Rabbit, they were accompanied by four very young students. I thought Clonfert House only housed the most senior students, but these four were teenagers. They seem to have been invited there intentionally, although they were ordered not to speak."

General Ah Puch also found this curious. Sesimite was correct that Clonfert House was open only to the most senior and advanced students. Had some new strain of enchanter been developed? Why would four teenagers, who should still be in one of the lower academies, be at Clonfert House, let alone present at the capture of Uncle Rabbit? The general needed more information about them.

"Sesimite, you must return and gather more information about those four young students. I'm not sure why, but their presence at the capture of Uncle Rabbit must mean something. We must accelerate everything now. If Adena finds out that we are behind Uncle Rabbit's actions, all of us will be in jeopardy of losing our lives. She does not tolerate disloyalty or deceit. Surely, this is what we have done."

"But, general," Sesimite was about to argue with General Ah Puch's decisions. "Shouldn't the other generals be involved now too?"

General Ah Puch snapped at Sesimite. "They will be. That's for me to address, not you. You do what I ordered. Leave now and do not return until you can tell me who the four students are and what has happened to Uncle Rabbit."

Sesimite noticed that General Ah Puch failed to order him to do the very thing they went to Confer House to discover—the identity of Adena's spy. Why? Had he forgotten about the spy? The general must be really afraid.

"General, what about the spy?"

"If you can find out who it is, then so do, but with the capture of Uncle Rabbit, we are in serious trouble. Unless we have some information for Adena that she is not expecting, we have nothing to bargain with. One more thing, Sesimite. Don't even think of running away. I will have eyes on you. Now, get out. Go back to Clonfert House. Find the answers to my questions."

General Ah Puch sat behind his desk. These events at Clonfert House could not be understated. The capture of Uncle Rabbit was dangerous. What if he told the headmaster everything he knew? After all, he was just a lesser animal spirit. The general regretted what they had done, but it could not be undone now. He needed to think.

"Yes, sir." Sesimite stepped through the flaps of the tent. He surveyed the number of squads' training. War was certainly at hand. What choices did he have? He could run away. Eyes on him or not, he could escape. If he did, how long before Adena came looking for him? Then what? He could go to Adena now and expose everything the generals had done. However, under no circumstances would he be able to claim innocence or manipulation at their hands. Adena knew he was too smart for that. Adena could be bargained with if one had something she wanted. That very thing was at Clonfert House—Uncle Rabbit. He chose to follow General Ah Puch's orders. Sesimite shifted once again to the shape of a fly. He headed back to Clonfert House. He would not leave until he discovered Uncle Rabbit's fate, why the four junior students were involved, and the identity of the spy. Unfortunately, he would not succeed in finding the truth.

*

General Ah Puch was deeply troubled. He and the other two generals had hatched a plan to go behind Adena's back.

Even though they could argue that the plan made sense strategically, it was obviously disloyal. It was also obvious that they had a high level of mistrust of Adena and her plans, even though they didn't know the specifics of that plan. That was where the threat to them lay. Mistakes she tolerated, but never mistrust of her, her intentions, or her actions. For just a brief moment, he considered that maybe Adena didn't know it was them who had sent Uncle Rabbit and Sesimite. After all, Sesimite wasn't sure of Uncle Rabbit's fate. How far would the headmaster go to extract information from Uncle Rabbit? How strong was Uncle Rabbit's ability to resist? He could only hope that Sesimite would return quickly with answers.

And what of those four junior students? What could their presence possibly mean? The spy. Who was the spy? Was that person a spy or a decoy planted by the magisterium? Without having the answers to these questions, they could not evaluate the feasibility of Adena's plans whatever they were. There were too many variables. As a general, he eliminated variables as much as possible before acting. He needed to consult with Generals Votan and Cabrakan.

"Guard," he called out. "Bring me one of our swiftest heralds."

"Yes, sir."

While General Ah Puch waited for the herald to arrive, he pulled a ground plan of Clonfert House from a chest.

A knocker, a type of fairy who worked in the mines, stepped into General Ah Puch's tent.

"Guard said you need a swift herald."

General Ah Puch looked up again from the chart.

"A knocker? They sent me a knocker?"

"Suit yourself, general. You'll find no one swifter than me."

"I thought you knockers were restricted to the mines. Aren't you extracting the mineral we need to make our armaments?"

"Mostly that's true, but I'm not fond of the mines. Hate them actually. I prefer sunshine and fresh air. One of your captains took a liking to me and sends me here and there on errands. Says not a sprite faster than me."

General Ah Puch looked the little knocker over again.

"Alright then. Do you know the location of General Votan's and Cabrakan's camps?"

"I most certainly do," the knocker boasted.

"Go now and tell them they are needed here without any delay."

The knocker then overstepped his place. "What shall I tell them is the urgency? Surely they'll ask me."

General Ah Puch threw his pen on the table. "Listen to me, you gnat. You just tell them they are needed here now. That is all you need to know."

"Okay, okay." The knocker was about to set off. "But call me a gnat again…"

He laughed and was gone.

It took the knocker three hours to notify the two generals. Each of them set out immediately with a small band of soldiers to head to General Ah Puch's encampment. They would reach it early tomorrow evening.

*

Not soon after the knocker was dispatched, the messenger arrived from Adena at General Ah Puch's camp.. It was a terse message to present himself before her in two days. That was all the messenger said. There was no direct threat, but a threat was there nonetheless. He wondered if the other generals had likewise been summoned. Tomorrow he would know.

Generals Votan and Cabrakan also received a message summoning them to Adena's court. They hoped General Ah Puch would know why. They had to move quickly if they were to meet with General Ah Puch and make it to Adena's court on time.

Chapter Eighteen

Galway, Ireland
At Clonfert House

Clonfert House was chaotic. The professors were gathered with the headmaster. Senior students were all abuzz over the sudden call for a general assembly. Michael, Minda, Kevin, and Affey were sequestered in their rooms, although it didn't keep them from trying to find a way out. Minda had convinced them that they needed to be where the action was. Affey objected, but not too strongly. They all wished they could attend the general assembly.

The headmaster first summoned the entire professional staff into the Scholars' Hall. He entered the hall in a hurry with Professors Mbaye, Howenstein, Smiley, and Mbaye in tow. His call to order could barely be heard above the murmurs of the staff.

"My dear colleagues, please settle down. We don't have much time and there is a lot to tell you. I must insist that we follow Rule Twenty-Seven and abstain from question or discussion until I have finished. Then, we will entertain questions for a brief time. My apologies that we are not following our normal collegiality, but when you hear what I have to say, you will understand."

The headmaster then explained, "Adena has embedded a spy in our midst. Another spy, most likely also from Adena's camp had recently been captured. He is known by the name of Uncle Rabbit." Uncle Rabbit's name swirled around the hall. "We believe he may have had an accomplice who escaped. Unfortunately, Uncle Rabbit refused to cooperate. He is now in the hands of the Green Maiden." Voices could be heard saying, "Oh no." They knew what it meant.

The headmaster continued, "We believe that Adena is plotting another war to steal the scrolls. We have no idea if or how much damage the spy has caused. We assume this spy is not one of you. Several voices shouted out, 'Assume! Assume! What do you mean assume?'"

"A poor choice of words on my part," said the headmaster. "None of you is a suspect. We believe that the spy is a senior student."

Someone shouted out, "What about those four junior students who are here?"

This presented a dilemma for the headmaster. He had to tell them something, but should he tell them all? Professor Howenstein stepped forward to save the headmaster.

"These four minor academy students have been identified as prodigies. They were brought here to be assessed. Professor O'Riley is mentoring them as well as monitoring them. We have placed them apart from the other students so that they are not distracted. It is unfortunate that they are present during this crisis, but it is best they remain with us for now."

The headmaster was relieved. Professor Howenstein's explanation satisfied the assembled staff.

Professor Mbaye spoke next. "We believe that the capture of Uncle Rabbit will accelerate Adena's plans. Since we think she may launch an initial foray soon to test our defenses, we don't have much time to prepare. We are asking each of you to gather those senior students in your care whose powers can be arranged around the perimeter of Clonfert House to defend it. You all know the protocols. The five of us up here will fortify the subterranean passages. Professor O'Riley is already preparing to take the scrolls to their emergency shelter."

The headmaster took over. "We will now bring in the senior students and share all of this with them. I ask that each of you find a place along the walls so you can observe your students. One of them is Adena's spy. Look for any reaction that is noteworthy. Also, check to see if any students under your charge are absent. If anyone is missing, notify me personally after the students are dismissed to meet you to set our defenses. Now, any questions?"

One of the newest additions to the professorial staff, Professor Rounder, asked the only question.

"Have we sent envoys to the spirit and fairy tribes soliciting their help?" The question was important.

The headmaster replied, "We have. We have also made a special request to Major Lisset. She and her women have remained loosely aligned with the west but have maintained a channel of communication with us. We await her response. We expect she will remain neutral." The headmaster looked around for any other questions. There were none.

"Let's bring in the senior students."

The students filed in silently. For many, this was the first time a general assembly included the entire professorial staff. Something special was happening.

Just as he had reviewed events with the professorial staff, the headmaster and the others explained what was happening. The only thing they deliberately left out was the presence of a spy among them. No questions were permitted. The students were dismissed to meet with their professor mentors to set the defenses of Clonfert House.

Once the last student had left, the headmaster asked if any student was missing. Every student was accounted for. Three professors indicated odd reactions in one of their students. The headmaster made note of who they were. Then they all departed to their various tasks.

*

Back in the study room of their hall, Michael, Minda, Kevin, and Affey argued over what they should do. Michael, the most cautious of the four, argued for staying put and doing exactly as they were told. The more complicated things became, the more Michael wanted to withdraw. Kevin listened to each of the others but was indecisive. Minda was determined that they were not going to stay shut off from the events unfolding around them. She couldn't decide if she wanted them to locate the scrolls once and for all or to ferret out the spy. Affey didn't say much at first, but when Minda paused to fashion a new argument, Affey spoke up.

"I have listened to all the three of you have said. As I see it, there is only one course of action."

The three of them were taken aback by Affey's sudden confidence. It was unlike her to voice an opinion on anything. She had always been content to follow Minda's lead. What the others didn't know, and what she wasn't going to tell them, was that her time with the Green Maiden, though brief, had changed her. She would never share the particulars with the others, but the Green Maiden had made clear to Affey that she, and she alone, would lead the others through the trials that lay ahead of them. For a reason Affey could not fathom, she accepted what the Green Maiden said. It must have been something about the way the Green Maiden told her that had such a profound effect on her. Minda was the most shocked by the change in her sister.

"Affey, what has come over you?"

"I'm not sure I can explain it," Affey said quietly. "Since my brief time with the Green Maiden, I am different somehow. Maybe someday I will know how and why. For now, I must follow what my consciousness tells me."

Kevin chimed in first, "What does your consciousness tell you we should do, Affey?"

Without any hesitation, she said, "We have but one clear path. First, I must ask you all a question. Did any of you see anything, spirit, fairy, elf, sprite, anything accompanying Uncle Rabbit?"

Michael thought he saw something, but now he wasn't so sure. Neither Minda nor Kevin remembered seeing anything. Their memories were affected by the spell the headmaster had cast over them in the cellar.

Michael told Affey, "I was supposed to locate two rabbits working together, which I did. But once everything started happening in the cellar of the cathedral, I only saw one rabbit. There may have been another rabbit, but we never found one. So, I'm not sure."

Minda added, "I saw the same thing Michael did. Only I think there was another one with Uncle Rabbit."

Affey waited a minute and then said, "I wasn't there with you, but somehow I am convinced there was another one present with Uncle Rabbit and he, she, or it escaped somehow. Let's put that aside for now. We have one goal. We must discover the identity of the spy. If there was someone who escaped, there is nothing we can do about it now."

Minda wasn't convinced. "Affey, what about what's happening all around us? It feels like Clonfert House is under siege. Shouldn't we help?"

Affey remained poised. "It is under siege or soon will be. We are just junior students no matter how advanced our powers might be. If we can identify the spy, then we will have something to offer that could turn the tide and maybe avoid any conflict."

The other three looked at one another for some indication of their responses to Affey.

"Affey," Minda started, "how do you propose we do this?"

Once again, Affey was poised and confident. "First, we must agree to ignore the rule forbidding the use of our powers on any other enchanter. The spy has surrendered that protection. I am suggesting we harness our four powers to probe the consciousness of every other student here."

Kevin interrupted her, "Wait, only one student is a spy. We can't probe every student here. It's taboo."

Michael added his voice, "I can't agree to this."

Minda offered a possible solution.

"Seems to me that the spy's thinking will be clouded. The spy has to be worried about being caught. Their mind won't be sharp or bright like the others. I propose that as soon as we encounter a bright, clear mind, we move on. Agreed?"

They all were in agreement, though Michael still had reservations.

They looked at Affey for her approval. "That is the best we can do."

Michael spoke up again. "How do we do this? Do you have any idea?"

Affey did. "I do, Michael, but it will require each of us to do something we've not done before. We must become a single point of consciousness. We must blend as if one."

Michael shared what happened earlier with Minda. "Well, I know that Minda can share mine. We did it during the events at the cathedral." Minda wasn't sure if what Michael said was a compliment or a slight. Michael said it as a matter of fact.

"Kevin?" Affey asked.

"Sure. I'm game. Don't have a clue how, but I'm in."

Affey remained still, the same stillness she experienced when she implemented chaos. Kevin felt it first.

"Oh, Affey, is this it?"

"Yes," was all she said.

Michael had released any obstacles as soon as Affey suggested a single-consciousness.

"Michael," Affey said. "You are with Kevin and me now. Minda?"

Minda was trying to join the single-consciousness, but there was something blocking her joining. Affey helped.

"Minda," she said, "I am your sister. I love you more than anything in the world."

That was enough. Minda was now aligned. They were as one—a single point of consciousness.

"Okay," Affey instructed, "let's start with the most senior students."

*

All through Clonfert House, the professors directed their students on setting the defenses. They had drilled many, many times for an event such as this, but this time, it was not a drill. Adena's forces were on the move. Meanwhile, in the depths below Clonfert House and Saint Brendan's Cathedral, the headmaster, together with Professors Smiley, Carakova, Mbaye, and Howenstein, sealed all access to the tunnels and crypts. They checked and double-checked one another. When they were satisfied that all was secure, they returned to the headmaster's chambers.

*

Pyx was back in her room, caught in utter panic. She was trapped. No doubt she thought someone somewhere would start probing her intentions. It was what she would do. They were probably scanning everyone's intentions.

How could she protect herself? She had to notify Jerome. She summoned her sprite who arrived looking out of sorts.

"What's wrong with you?" Pyx asked.

The sprite replied, "Have you any idea what's going on here? This is not going to turn out well. I need to get out of here and so should you."

"You know I can't leave. You must go to Jerome and tell him what has happened. I will understand if you don't return. In fact, don't come back. We might be discovered if you do."

"Pyx, I will try to return." The sprite flew out her window and sped towards the realm where Jerome was held.

Pyx couldn't remain in her room. By now, her mentor would have noticed her absence from the defense of Clonfert House. She made sure her room looked normal before she departed for her station at the southern defense. She reminded herself to keep her mind clear and bright. 'Don't let any thought other than the defense of Clonfert House enter my consciousness.' Try as she might, she feared she would fail.

Chapter Nineteen

The Western Quarter
The Generals Meet with Adena

The three generals, Ah Puch, Votan, and Cabrakan, met hastily at General Ah Puch's camp. They had been summoned to appear before Adena in less than twenty-four hours. It was almost a full day's journey away. Sesimite had not yet returned from Clonfert House, which left them in the dark about Uncle Rabbit's fate, or what, if anything, he had told the magisterium. They all agreed that Adena did not summon them so abruptly because she was pleased with them. Surely, they had been summoned to face her anger.

"We need a plan," General Votan said. There was fear in his voice.

General Cabrakan offered an alternative possibility.

"How do we know Adena is aware of anything? Especially, how could she possibly know that we sent Uncle Rabbit and Sesimite to Clonfert House? She has many detractors who would like to see her fall from her throne. She has always said we are her most loyal and trustworthy colleagues. Perhaps, she has summoned us because she wants to move on Clonfert House now. Maybe she didn't trust anyone enough to send us that message, so she wants to deliver it herself."

General Votan was skeptical. "Adena has spies everywhere. We've been very careful, but there is a real risk here."

"We must approach her as if everything is normal. We will just have to wait and see what her mood is. If she accuses us, then we will just deny it." General Ah Puch was confident in his suggestion.

"What if she has proof?" General Votan asked.

General Ah Puch was growing impatient. They needed to get moving. "Then let her show it. She will reveal everything as soon as we arrive. If she's enraged, she won't be able to hold back. One sign that we are in trouble will be the number of guards surrounding her. If there are more than her usual retinue, then we should take it that we are about to be arrested. If not, then I venture we are beyond suspicion and she has another agenda. I wish Sesimite would return. Hopefully, he will find us on our way to Adena."

General Votan interrupted him, "If we don't depart now, we will arrive late. That in itself will make her angry."

General Cabrakan offered one last suggestion before they left. "If and when Sesimite returns, we must cage him. We can't risk him running off to Adena. Agreed?"

They all agreed. General Ah Puch ordered the Inescapable Dragon Goal to be loaded on a cart that they would take with them. No creature, even a shape-shifter, had ever escaped from the Inescapable Dragon Goal. The three generals, together with the cart carrying the Goal and a small number of soldiers, departed for Adena's camp.

*

Sesimite remained in the form of an insect while at Clonfert House. He only spent an hour or so there because he was anxious without Uncle Rabbit by his side.

He was first struck by the level of activity he saw. Professors and students seemed to be preparing some sort of defense. 'Why?' he wondered. 'Could it be that once again Clonfert House knew of Adena's plans as they had in the past? Did this mean that Adena's spy was not a spy at all, but an agent of Clonfert House?' Then a terrible thought occurred to him. 'What if Uncle Rabbit told them everything?' Sesimite didn't think so. That was, unless they tortured Uncle Rabbit. Uncle Rabbit bragged about his ability to hold his tongue, but had he ever been really tested? Uncle Rabbit was fiercely loyal as far as Sesimite knew. 'So, no, Uncle Rabbit wouldn't...but torture can turn anyone. What about those four young students who were in the basement? Why were they there? What did it mean?' There was no time for Sesimite to search for the answers. He just had to do the best he could.

First, he checked the breach in the foundation to Saint Brendan's Cathedral. It was sealed shut. He flittered around as much as he thought prudent, looking for Uncle Rabbit. There was no sign of him. The spy—could he find out who it was? No! There was no way Sesimite could think of to identify the spy. There was nothing more he could do at Clonfert House. He must return and inform the generals of what he discovered.

The path back to General Ah Puch's camp intersected with the path leading to Adena's camp. At the intersection, he came upon the three generals. He shape-shifted into his usual giant form to block their way.

"Sesimite, so glad to see you. We are on our way to Adena's camp. What did you find at Clonfert House?" General Ah Puch asked.

Sesimite, now in the form of a rabbit, told them about everything he saw.

"Thank you, Sesimite. This was not an easy task for you," Cabrakan said.

Sesimite bowed to the three generals. As he did, he was seized and thrown into the Inescapable Dragon Goal. Sesimite knew all about the Goal. His brother, the western hill giant, Thaxis, was thrown into one many eons ago for trying to hunt in the Leprechaun's sacred forest. They eventually released him. He was never the same after that. Sesimite could not figure out why they had done this to him. Hopefully, it was for his own protection, since Uncle Rabbit's fate was unknown. He would just have to wait and see. They left Sesimite in the Goal, hidden along the edge of the road. They would get back to him later.

When they arrived at Adena's camp, they didn't notice any unusual assembly of guards. They were led immediately to Adena's throne where she was waiting for them. They noted that the usual number of guards were present, as were the two manticores flanking her throne. The three generals kneeled in front her as a sign of respect. They waited for her to speak before they rose. General Ah Puch looked up briefly. Adena was tapping her nails on the arms of her throne. Her eyes flashed with anger. Then she spoke. She wasted no time getting to the point.

"We have a traitor among us. Someone has sent that creature, Uncle Rabbit, to Clonfert House. I don't know the reason why, but I will find out. He has been captured. He was taken to the Pillory at the Weeping Cross. He is at this moment, no doubt, being interrogated. He is a weak creature. Known to be for sale to the highest bidder. He's also a coward. Whatever he knows, he will tell them. I also think it is entirely possible he was sent there to warn Clonfert House of our plans. Such an act is treason. An act of treason worthy of death."

General Votan rose to speak, but Adena was not having any of it.

"I'm not asking for your advice. That goes for the two of you also. I have my way of finding out and I will find out who this traitor is. I will deal them myself. My spy at Clonfert House continues to relay intelligence that my plans have not been compromised."

"If I may, mistress," General Ah Puch said as he stood up. He was going to tell her a lie, since he was fairly certain Uncle Rabbit had told them of her plans since Clonfert House was in a defensive posture. He had to lie to save them.

"Perhaps Uncle Rabbit wasn't sent there at all. Maybe, he went of his own accord?" General Ah Puch thought the risk was worth it, since there was little chance Uncle Rabbit would ever be released by Clonfert House.

This had some appeal for Adena. Yet, she was skeptical. "For what purpose?"

"That I do not know," General Ah Puch said. "I just think that jumping to conclusions about traitors and treason may lead you to the wrong person." General Ah Puch was pushing the limits of her patience, but he felt he had no choice.

Adena dismissed his suggestion. "There is a traitor and I know it. Someone wants to derail us from stealing the scrolls, or they want my throne. I don't much care which it is. Neither one will happen." She rose from her throne, stepped off the platform, and came face-to-face with the three generals. They kneeled before her. "Our attack on Clonfert House will come as a surprise. They will not be prepared for us this time. It's time to crush Clonfert House once and for all."

The three generals were cornered. They knew the defenses were already set at Clonfert House. They couldn't tell her how they knew. It would reveal that Uncle Rabbit had an accomplice who reported to them and not her. They remained kneeling, waiting for what came next.

"Generals. We will assemble on the heath on the outskirts of Clonfert House in twenty-four hours. We are on the threshold of victory. Our losses will be light, which should relive you of your concerns." She left with her manticores behind her trying to catch-up.

The journey back to their respective camps was filled with dread. Each of the generals was keenly aware that they would be leading their legions into a trap. It would be just like the last time. How could they both fulfill Adena's orders and protect their armies from defeat? There was no clear solution they could see. They could only hope Adena would have a change of heart once she saw Clonfert House poised to defend against her attack.

On the way back to their training camp, the generals released Sesimite from the Inescapable Dragon's Goal.

They imposed one condition on his release. He was to be exiled to the Barren Island. If he ever set off the island, he would be executed. Sesimite agreed and reached the Barren Island early the next morning. It would take some time before he dared venture off the island.

*

Jerome received the message from Pyx's sprite. The sprite emphasized that Clonfert Hosue had set its defenses against an imminent attack. She also made certain that Jerome took note of the presence of Affey, Michael, Minda, and Kevin. Pyx had told her to do so, though she gave no explanation or further instruction with regard to the four. Jerome immediately dispatched a messenger to Adena that she must contact him without delay. He had urgent news.

Adena was so caught up in her rage over the presence of a traitor that she sent the messenger back with a terse response. "I'm too busy right now. I'm on the cusp of victory. I will come after."

Jerome forced the messenger to return to Adena to tell her this was news that would affect her victory.

When the messenger arrived, Adena's camp was on full battle-ready. They were beginning to march off. Adena refused to even see the messenger. Adena's guards tried to arrest the messenger, but she escaped. She flew to Jerome. He had done all he could. It wouldn't matter in the end. Adena would find him at fault and punish him. There was nothing he could do. His fate was in her hands just as it always had been.

At dawn the next morning, Adena marched to the heath on the outskirts of Clonfert House to assure that this time, victory was hers. The scrolls would be hers to control.

Chapter Twenty

Galway, Ireland
Clonfert House
Awaiting Adena's Arrival

While Clonfert House propped up its defenses, the headmaster had sent a message to Major Lisset, urging she and her women to join the battle to protect the scrolls. Major Lisset responded that she and her troops would remain apart from this battle. She gave no reason why. The headmaster sent final word that he hoped if things turned dire for Clonfert House and the scrolls, she would come to their aid. He didn't expect a reply and did not get one. From her distant encampment at the Doon Well, Major Lisset kept watch just the same. She would not let the scrolls slip into Adena's hands. Major Lisset also kept counsel with the Green Maiden who was her longtime confidant.

The headmaster took up a position on the western defensive tower. From this vantage point, he could see when Adena's forces approached. The other professors monitored the other defenses and rotated the watch to keep them fresh. They didn't want to get caught by surprise.

In the chaos surrounding the preparations for war, Affey, Michael, Minda, and Kevin were left unsupervised. Their mentors assumed they would stay put as they were told. Only Gianni Giannotti checked on them once to see if they needed anything to eat. He was in such a hurry that he really didn't give them time to answer. He seemed genuinely scared. Other than Gianni, no one paid them any attention at all. They thought this odd, given the circumstances of their being at Clonfert House and their participation in the capture of Uncle Rabbit.

As they agreed, once they were of a single-consciousness, they began to sweep through the minds of the students at Clonfert House. They had no idea if their probing would be felt or gone unnoticed. They hoped that the preparation for war would be something of a distraction. Of a more serious concern was whether their professors were monitoring them. If that turned out to be the case, then they didn't know what would happen. They set aside their concerns and kept to their task. If they could identify the spy and capture whoever it was, the information the spy would provide might just give Clonfert House a distinct advantage in this fight.

As they swept over the minds of Clonfert House, one student after another revealed minds that were clear, bright, and focused on what lay ahead. Even though they only probed briefly, they were amazed at the depths of the senior students' composure in light of what they were about to face. Every student they encountered was braced for conflict, their powers twitching to be released.

After several hours, Minda suggested that they take a break. Michael and Kevin went to get refreshments. Minda sat with her arm around Affey. It was the first time they were alone and could talk.

"Whatever has happened to you, Affey? Whatever it was has made you more powerful than I ever imagined. I'm proud of you." Minda held her sister a little tighter.

Affey leaned against her sister. "Minda, this is exhausting. It takes so much energy. I feel completely drained sometimes. I have noticed that my emotional response is completely different than it used to be. I feel relaxed. I'm not anxious. I just wish my physical reaction was more like my emotional one. Thank you for being proud of me. I have always been proud of you—of us. This is different now. I have to work a little on my own. We are doing good. You have to trust me."

"I do trust you, Affey." Michael and Kevin returned with a tray of snacks.

"How are you doing, Affey?" Kevin asked, setting the tray down closest to her.

Though they were working as one, Affey was the center holding them together. It was what was sapping her strength.

"I'm fine, Kevin. Thank you for asking." Affey reached down to get a cookie. She closed her eyes to rest.

Minda noticed that Michael seemed to be drifting of. "Are you okay, Michael?"

"I guess." Michael wasn't sure how much he should say. "I'm still not comfortable with what we are doing. I support it though. I just hope I'm not a hindrance."

Affey opened her eyes. "You are not, Michael." She indicated that they should reform their circle and get back to finding the spy.

They easily rejoined their shared consciousness which came as no surprise to Affey. The Green Maiden taught her how to make it work.

They scanned eight more students before they landed on Pyx. Pyx was much less focused than any of the other students. Pyx was not emanating much energy. Minda said what they all were thinking, "It's her."

Affey released them from the single-consciousness. "We must go to her now."

"Wait!" Kevin shouted. "Shouldn't we tell the headmaster or someone in charge?"

Affey stood up. "No! We will go and grab her now. We will bring her here."

Minda did not agree. "Why would we bring her here? If we do manage to capture her, which I have my doubts about since she is senior student with skills beyond our own, what are we supposed to do with her then? Shouldn't we just take her to the headmaster?"

Affey's determination was not to be shaken. "It's quite simple. We were brought here for the specific purpose of defending the scrolls. Remember what Master Chan Wu said. Remember the files we have all read. We four alone have the power needed to ultimately protect the scrolls. What we have just done is exactly what they want us to do. I believe that even if we went to the headmaster, he would tell us to do this anyway. So, we are going to go and capture Pyx. Her powers are limited right now because she is afraid of being caught. The advantage is ours. We will bring her here, extract everything from her, and then we will take her and her information to the headmaster."

Minda had one more observation. "Master Chan Wu has been watching over us. Don't you think he'll know what we are up to and will stop us?"

Once again, Affey had an answer. "If he is, which I doubt, since he is as distracted as the others, then he knows we are doing what we were brought here to do. He won't interfere."

Michael wanted to add his opinion. "What about Professor O'Riley? Don't we owe it to him?"

Affey stood perfectly still. No one moved. In this singular moment, she realized she was their leader. The ultimate fate of the scrolls rested with her. She needed them, but they had to follow her. There was no more time for discussion. Yet, maybe Michael had a point.

"Alright, let's go to the library and tell him." She led them out of the room towards the library. There, they were met with a surprise. Master Chan Wu was waiting at the door for them.

"Well, I was expecting you a little sooner, but at last you are here. Surprised to see me?" They all nodded. Even Affey didn't see this coming. "Just a few minutes ago, you were all quite chatty about your plans and now you are all tongue-tied?" Master Chan Wu chuckled.

"Then you know what we've been doing?" Minda asked. Master Chan Wu chuckled again. He then stepped close to Affey.

"You have evolved since your time with the Green Maiden, haven't you? Oh yes, I know all about that. Very proud of you I am." He then addressed all of them. "I told you from the very start that I would be watching over you. I never break a promise. Ever. Now, come with me."

Master Chan Wu opened the door to the library. They all sat around the table once again.

Michael spoke first. "Master, you know then that we have identified the spy and intend to capture her and then interrogate her."

Master Chan Wu chuckled again. "Oh, Michael, how determined you now are. I do know everything. When will you get that through your thick skull? You all must listen to Affey. She was correct when she said that if you were to have come to me first, I would have asked you to do exactly what you are doing. What you are able to do can only be done by the four of you. It's why you were brought here. You will now follow Affey. Go and take Pyx. Instead of bringing her back to your rooms, you will bring her here. It's safer here. I will be nearby just in case something goes wrong, which I don't think will happen. There is also a secret room here in the library that can block any possibility of outside influence as you talk to her. Now go. Bring her here. You will not have any trouble apprehending her."

Minda asked, "Will Professor O'Riley also be here with us?"

"No, he will not. He is preparing to secret away the scrolls with the guardians." Master Chan Wu's mention of the guardians came as a surprise. He had never mentioned them before.

"Guardians?" Affey asked.

"Yes, there are guardians we can all on from the fairy kingdoms in times such as these," Master Chan Wu explained. Just then, Professor O'Riley appeared from out of the shadows.

"I would like the four of you to come with me for a minute. There is something I want to show you." The four of them followed Professor O'Riley to yet another part of the library they had never seen. He stopped briefly before a heavy iron door etched with runes. "What you are about to see, few here get to see. It's time you caught a glimpse of what you are sworn to protect." With that, he swung open the iron door.

In the middle of the room was a large chest covered in runes similar to the ones on the iron door. It had an inner glow that illuminated the rest of the room. Surrounding the chest were a cadre of creatures of various sizes, shapes, and colors. Some had wings. Some were beautiful, Some were not. A few snarled when they entered. A few others looked at the four of them with a sense of wonder. Professor O'Riley then introduced each of the students by name.

"This is Michael. This is Kevin. These two girls are the twins, Minda and Affey." The mention of 'twins' brought gasps from several of the guardians. Twins were thought by the fairy world to possess special talents rarely encountered. "This one is named Minda. This is Affey." At the mention of Affey's name, five of the smallest winged creatures swooped in close to her. They hovered in front of her, examining every aspect of her face. One of them, a blue green imp, reached out and touched her cheek. They fairies laughed and returned to their perches.

"What was that all about?" Minda asked.

"Affey's reputation is growing, Minda. Even the fairies have heard about Affey. Now, off you go. It's time for Pyx to be taken."

Professor O'Riley led them back into the library, closing the door behind him. "When you return, I, the guardians, and the scrolls will be gone. We must go into hiding until this battle with Adena is over. When it is, I will return. Do what Affey asks of you. And don't forget that Master Chan Wu is looking out for you. Those discs you all are carrying that I gave you? They will be of no use to you now, but keep them nonetheless. They may come in handy someday in the future." He turned and left them.

Master Chan Wu took them to the library door. "You must bring Pyx here. Do not take any other course of action. I am watching. When you return with her, I will show where to take her." He motioned for them to leave.

Affey led Michael, Minda, and Kevin directly to Pyx's room. They didn't ask her how she knew where it was. They had come to follow her without question. It was the one decision they each made without hesitation.

Chapter Twenty-One

Galway, Ireland
Clonfert House
Pyx's Room

Pyx decided her best option was to keep moving around. Word had reached her that prefects, such as her, had been released from their usual duty stations and were to wander around, encouraging the others on duty or to find relief for those who needed it. By wandering around, she would be seen as fulfilling her duties. It would also give time to think about an escape. In all the activity, it might be easy for her to steal away. They wouldn't notice she was gone for a while. She went back to her room to prepare some things to take with her. Just as she turned the corner near her room, Affey and the others approached her.

Affey had planned a ruse to trick Pyx into coming with them. She hoped Pyx was afraid enough of being discovered as the spy that she would go along with the ruse.

Affey went directly to Pyx and said, "Are you the prefect whose name is Mistress Pyx?"

This put Pyx on edge, which was just what Affey expected. Pyx kept to herself. So, how did these four junior students know who she was?

She stared down at Affey. "Who wants to know?"

Affey stared right back up at her. "Professor O'Riley, who is our mentor, said that there is something special in the library he needs help with. Something about runes and that you were one of the only students who could help him decipher them. He asked us to find you and bring you to the library at once."

Pyx summoned her powers of thought-reading, but it couldn't penetrate into Affey. She tried the others with the same result. She then tried to thought-bend. Same result came. 'Why is this not working?' she thought.

"Mistress Pyx, that will not work on us." That was all Affey said. Pyx didn't seem to hear her.

"Rune interpretation you said?"

"Yes, mistress, that is what he said," Affey responded.

Pyx had had several encounters with Professor O'Riley over rune translations. There was one particular occasion when, during a library orientation in her first year, she happened to pick up a large manuscript from one of the shelves marked *'Tuatha De Danaan.'* Professor O'Riley noticed and asked her why she had picked up that particular manuscript. She said she wasn't sure. He then asked if she could read it. To her surprise, she could, although she had never encountered runes like them before. He had her bring the manuscript to him. He opened the book randomly and pointed to a section. She translated it perfectly. It read, *"To those who read these sacred runes, who come to know their wisdom, know also their danger."* Professor O'Riley told her to return the manuscript to the shelf. A year later, Professor O'Riley summoned her again. He had her translate another manuscript of similar runes entitled, *'Field Guide to the Hillocks of Brittany.'* It was just a geography text. She couldn't understand why he has asked her to do the translation. She didn't ask and he never said. At this particular moment and under her circumstances, she couldn't refuse. If it was a trap, so be it.

"Can't we do this later? It's been a long day and I'm tired," she asked to no one in particular.

"Afraid not," Minda said. "If Professor O'Riley said to bring you now, it must be important."

"Alright, hopefully this won't take long and I can get back to room for some rest."

Pyx followed the four students to the library.

As soon as they entered the library, Master Chan Wu cast Pyx under a binding spell. Under this spell, she had little freedom of movement but could think and speak clearly. She was led into the secret room Master Chan Wu had mentioned earlier. She was forced into a chair by the same spell.

"What is this?" Pyx demanded. "Where is Professor O'Riley?"

Affey stood over Pyx. "We know who you are, Mistress Pyx."

Pyx once again tried to probe into the young minds in the room with her.

"I told you," Affey scolded Pyx, "that won't work on us."

"So, this is how it's going to be? You can use your powers on me, but I can't use mine on you? You must be aware that what you are doing is forbidden. You will be banished for this. You have no idea who you are dealing with." Pyx was defiant. Pyx thought this would put a stop to all of this. She was wrong.

Kevin then said, "We know exactly who you are, mistress. A spy!"

Affey continued on Kevin's words. "You are Adena's spy." At this point, the only thing that mattered was getting Pyx to tell them everything. Then Affey told a lie.

"Uncle Rabbit told us it was you. Now, you're going to tell us everything you have told Adena. You will leave nothing out. I will know. Trust me. I will know. You will explain to us exactly how you relayed this information to Adena."

Pyx refused to speak, but she was powerless to stop the stream of images that flashed though her mind. Try as she might, she could not stop them. This had never happened to her before. What power did these four have? What special power did this little girl standing before her have? Why could she not stop these images?

What played out in her mind for all of them to see were the minutest details of everything Pyx had done, every communication she had with Jerome, and her plans to escape. Everything came out. When the catalog of her activities finished playing out, she asked a single question of Affey.

"What happens now?"

Before Affey could answer, Master Chan Wu entered the room.

"Master Chan Wu," Pyx said, shocked to see him.

"Mistress Pyx, you too once had promise such as these four. Yet, here you are. What did Adena promise you? Riches? New powers? A realm of your own?" Master Chan Wu was more intense than the four students had ever seen him. "No, don't answer me. I don't care. You are going to leave us. Forever. You will not see this place or Adena ever again."

A swoosh filled the room. The Green Maiden appeared.

Master Chan Wu turned back to Pyx. "Let me introduce you to the Green Maiden. She has a special place waiting for you. You remember Uncle Rabbit? You are going to join him. Green Maiden, she is yours."

The Green Maiden swooped Pyx up and they vanished.

Master Chan Wu turned his attention back to the students who were astonished at how swiftly Master Chan Wu dealt with Pyx. They were just as astonished at the arrival of the Green Maiden.

"Your efforts will be chronicled in the history of Clonfert House. Now, I must insist that you return to your rooms and rest. You have done enough for one day. This time, you will remain there. I will be watching. Don't make me post guards," he said with a smile.

"Thank you, Master Chan Wu," Affey said on behalf of them all.

They returned to their rooms and quickly fell asleep. Strangely, none of them dreamed.

*

As night fell over Clonfert House, the professors made their rounds, reminding the senior students to keep their minds clear and bright. Tomorrow, they may very well be called upon to deploy their powers and physical might to defend Clonfert House. Just before the gong would chime the last watch of the night, the headmaster addressed all of Clonfert House through the loudspeaker system.

"To those professors who are new to us and never had to defend these walls. To all our students who have yet to face the threat we have faced for generations. I want to explain to you a particular obstacle we face.

"All of you have been trained in the martial arts, some in hand-to-hand combat, some with the bow, and others with sword. You have probably wondered why, since you have powers that would seemingly overcome any physical threat. You may be confused as to why we have supplied these instruments of war to you as you prepare to defend this house. Let me explain.

"When fairy folk go to war against each other, there is always a moment when power versus power ends in stalemate. In other words, the powers cancel each other out, leaving physical conflict as the only recourse.

"With the advent of the modern age, with all of its benefits, there has also come the advent of weapons of immense cruelty. You all know what I'm talking about. Our fairy colleagues have always shunned modern weaponry in favor of the ancient way of battle. As war technology advanced to the point of mass destruction, the fairy kingdoms signed a treaty. That treaty limits the use of battle weaponry to the martial arts alone. No modern instruments of war are permitted. Not one of the fairy kingdoms has ever broken this treaty. In years since the treaty, the fairies haven't even attempted to use their powers against each other because they knew it was a waste of energy, energy they would need to muster for the physical battle. We at Clonfert House are also part of that treaty.

"We fully expect that is what will happen this time. This will be a physical fight. Adena remains a part of the fairy world. Despite her reputation, I don't think she would violate the treaty. Her generals would abandon her if she did.

"That being said, your first instinct will be to hurl your powers at Adena and her forces. Perhaps we should and will test their resolve. We will let you know if and when that time arrives. However, it is best you gird yourselves for a physical fight. We will prevail. Clonfert House will survive. The scrolls will remain safe with us.

"Until the dawn, rest as best you can. Be vigilant. This is what your families expect of you. It is what we must expect of ourselves. After tomorrow, your names will forever be engraved in the annals of this great house."

A hush fell over the ramparts of Clonfert House. Some students felt fear for the first time. The professors who mentored them quickly moved in to reassure them. At last, the tension eased. All were ready to defend Clonfert House.

*

A lookout posted on the western turret sent word to the headmaster that an array of torches was moving along the horizon. The evening bird song stopped. A lone opossum's eyes glowed red at the edge of the forest. All along the defenses, the senior students kept their minds clear and bright. They stretched to keep their muscles limber for the upcoming fight. Each one of them felt some fear. Yet, their years of training led them to this moment. The entire history of Clonfert House was about to be tested. They resolved not to fail.

The headmaster and the professorial staff gathered in the Scholars' Hall to recite the ancient rites for victory.

Professor O'Riley and the guardians were secreted away in Bronwyn's Vault, the only place they knew the scrolls would be safe. Professor O'Riley recited the ancient ritual for protection.

In a few hours, dawn would break.

Chapter Twenty-Two

Galway, Ireland
Adena's Encampment on the Heath
On the Outskirts of Clonfert House

As they traveled to meet Adena on the heath, Generals Ah Puch, Votan, and Cabrakan discussed various schemes to keep Adena from discovering their role in Uncle Rabbit's presence at Clonfert House. However, when they arrived at the heath, the more immediate worry was the imminent battle. Adena was sure their arrival would catch Clonfert House unprepared. Her confidence in victory consumed her. They could not figure out any way to warn her or convince her to reconsider without exposing themselves. They also talked at length about the duty to their troops and how leading them into this battle was a betrayal. What choice did they have? They would be sacrificed just like everyone else. General Votan expressed a hope that some last-minute event would forestall the fight.

Adena was waiting for them when they arrived.

"To my tent. Now."

They followed her without question. Inside the tent, she turned on them, furious.

"You should have arrived before I did. The heath should have been secured, the watch set. Instead, I arrive to find an empty, exposed terrain. This is a serious breach of your duties. I will deal with it later. For now, let me tell you what I expect of you."

The three generals said nothing.

"An hour before dawn, each of you will lead a small expeditionary team towards Clonfert House. This will be done under the cover of the pre-dawn darkness. You will approach from all directions. You are to examine the ramparts to see if there are any signs of particular weakness. Each of you will then report to me with a plan of attack for the segment you explored. You must be prepared to initiate your attack immediately. We must catch them off-guard and we will. Now, get out." She left them no room to speak.

Once they were out of earshot, the three generals spoke briefly. They didn't have much time.

"This might be our chance. If we tell her we saw the defenses set, she'll have to abandon her plan. She will have lost the element of surprise," was General Ah Puch's idea.

General Cabrakan wasn't convinced. "If we tell her that, who knows where her rage will take her?"

"I agree," said General Votan. "We are in a terrible position. Let's just do what she asked us to do. We're in this far already. We have no way out of this."

Each of them went off to gather a small troop. In the hour before dawn, they approached Clonfert House.

The lookout on the western turret, who had the gift of night sight, saw the movement of the troops coming towards Clonfert House. He notified the headmaster, who came to the turret with Professor Mbaye.

"There," indicated the lookout, "and there, there, and there. They are approaching from all directions."

Neither the headmaster nor Professor Mbaye could see them.

"How many?" asked Professor Mbaye.

"Five in each troop."

"Keep tracking them," ordered the headmaster. "I will be right back. Professor Mbaye, please come with me."

The headmaster explained to Professor Mbaye, "This is most fortunate. We have an opportunity to knock Adena off her game. She doesn't have any idea we are ready for her. She thinks her attack will be a surprise. The last thing she wants is a repeat of her last defeat. It would mean the end of her reign. She would be overthrown for sure. We are going to capture these troops. When they don't return, she won't be able to contain her rage. She will lose control, lash out, and make mistakes."

"What is your plan?"

For many, many years, the headmaster selected several students to train directly with him. He was a master of several secret, very difficult martial arts. His students learned these from him. He also taught them the Way of Stealth. The Way of Stealth allowed them to move undetected. They could sneak up on anyone, human or spirit, and take them under their control. There was no defense to the Way of Stealth. These handpicked students never revealed to anyone their skill. Anonymity was drilled into them by the headmaster.

"I have my ways, professor. I need you to relay the lookout's information to me as he gets it. Just send me your thoughts. I will hear them."

Professor Mbaye returned to the western turret. She kept the headmaster abreast of all that the lookout saw.

The headmaster sent out a mind signal to all his Way of Stealth students. They met him at the Weeping Cross.

The headmaster said to them, "Your time has come. We are about to be probed by four expeditionary troops. Each troop has five members. They are coming from the east, west, north, and south. You will go in teams of three. Bind them and bring them to the Scholars' Hall. Any questions?"

The smallest of his students, a second-year student from Santa Fe, New Mexico, named Brenda, asked, "Can we do whatever is necessary?" Brenda was the one student who the headmaster had difficulty controlling.

"Don't hurt them. Otherwise, yes."

Brenda puffed up a little.

"Now, go." The headmaster opened the backdoor to the Scholars' Hall. They sped off to capture their prey. The headmaster returned to the western turret to watch events unfold.

"Headmaster," whispered the lookout, "the troop to the west has disappeared. Oh, and so did the southern troop. What does that mean?"

"Patience," whispered back the headmaster. "Soon the others will disappear too."

"Yes, yes, they're gone too. What the…?" the lookout started to speak louder.

The headmaster put his fingers to the lookout's mouth. "You will tell no one what you have seen. Do you understand? I will explain when the time is right. Just keep watch and let me know if anything else comes to your attention."

"Yes, sir."

The headmaster and Professor Mbaye went immediately to the Scholars' Hall. There, the three generals and their troops sat on the floor in chains. The students of The Way of Stealth surrounded them.

"Well, well, well. Look who we have here. Professor Mbaye, let me introduce you to Adena's three most trusted generals. You are General Ah Puch. Am I right?" asked the headmaster. Ah Puch nodded 'yes.'

"And you are Generals Votan and Cabrakan?" They too nodded 'yes.'

Without saying a word, the three generals knew their fate with Clonfert House might be better than with Adena. They did not defy the headmaster.

The headmaster did not give them any opportunity to speak, nor did he have much to say to them. There was nothing they could offer that he, the headmaster, didn't already know.

"Your troops will be released," the headmaster said. "They should not be punished for your failure of leadership. You three will be surrendered to the Green Maiden who is on her way here now for you. I suppose you know what that means?"

The generals did know what this meant for them. Still, it was a relief not to have to return to Adena.

The headmaster directed his students of The Way of Stealth to remain with the generals until the Green Maiden took them. It would not be long. After that, they were to return to their posts.

The headmaster then spoke to the troops he was releasing. "You are free to go. I would advise you to turn away from this fight. Do not return to Adena. It is best for you to disappear. She will hold you at fault and punish you. Her rage will know no boundaries. Professor Mbaye, please show them out."

Professor Mbaye led them all the way to the eastern exit. They fled in various directions. None of them returned to Adena's camp.

*

Adena paced the hillock on the heath, staring in the distance, waiting to see the expeditionary troops return. When the sun broke over the horizon, she was alarmed. There was no sign of the generals or their troops. Where had they gone? Did they abandon her? Did they get caught? If they were caught, that could only mean one thing—Clonfert House had been warned of her arrival.

She screamed. She screamed so loudly that the birds rushed from the trees, small creatures scattered for cover, and her entire encampment was terrified by the sound of her scream.

She screamed again, this time lower, longer, and more sinister. Her manticores fled into the forest.

"I have been betrayed. All of you shall feel the sting of my wrath." All the troops who had assembled on the heath just below her fell to the ground in terror. Her eyes were pitch-black. A wind swirled around her. She spread her arms wide, tilted her head to the sky, and screamed once again. This time, her scream became a monster itself. It engulfed her. It carried her up high into the sky. From above, she glared at Clonfert House. She wanted nothing more in this moment than to see Clonfert House in ruin.

The lookout saw what was happening and summoned the headmaster.

"Clear this turret and the entire western rampart. Do it now," the headmaster commanded. His voice carried over the entirety of Clonfert House. All went still. The headmaster took up a position on the top of the western turret. He alone had to face Adena.

As he ascended the turret, Adena followed his every move. He was the one who led her dismissal from Clonfert House. He was the one who stripped her of her powers. It was time he paid the price. She summoned all of her energy. She concentrated all her power to deliver a deadly blow to the headmaster. She spread her arms. The monstrous wind swirled around her. To anyone other than the headmaster, she would be indestructible.

On the turret, the headmaster stood stone-still. He watched Adena intently. He knew what she was going to do. He had taught it to her. It would take all of his own power to repel her. He would use it against her. It would destroy her once and for all.

Adena opened her mouth to let out one last scream. Just as she was about to direct her energy to the headmaster, an arrow pierced her throat. She clutched at it. Her eyes lightened. The monstrous wind collapsed. She fell to the ground.

"I know this arrow," she struggled to get out the words. There, approaching her, was Major Lisset. "You? You did this to me? Why?"

Major Lisset walked up to Adena who was struggling to stand up. "There is no place in this world for you, Adena. You want to keep us out of balance. I cannot allow that. We creatures of the wind and the woods must keep the world safe. You have always been a danger to that balance. No more."

Adena fell to her knees. Her breath was coming in short, difficult gasps. The two women stared at each other. Adena then fell face-down on the heath. Major Lisset felt Adena's throat. She was dead. The major extracted her arrow and shot it towards the western turret of Clonfert House, a sign that Adena was dead.

The headmaster had witnessed it all. He was shocked at Major Lisset's arrival and even more surprised at the action she took. He desperately wanted to know why. The major returned to her encampment at the Doon Well. It would be several generations before she would explain her actions to the headmaster.

Chapter Twenty-Three

Galway, Ireland
The General Assembly
Clonfert House

By the time Adena reached her end, it was mid-morning. The headmaster had sounded the alarm that all was clear and that Adena had abandoned the fight. He was saving the particulars for the general assembly.

Professor O'Riley, with the help of the guardians, returned the scared scrolls to their resting place. The guardians returned to their respective realms.

Affey, Michael, Minda, and Kevin were summoned to the general assembly to join everyone else.

All of Clonfert House was present. The headmaster stepped up to the podium and addressed the assembly.

"Today, we have turned away once again the ancient threat to our house and all it contains. The scrolls are safe. We are safe. It is only because of our undying commitment to the union of our realms, human and spirit, that we can keep the world of the wind and the woods in balance. Each and every one of you, without exception, has made this day possible. You have had to look deep within yourselves to find the courage and confidence to fight. This time you did not, but that does not mean you never will. It is the ever-present possibility of threat that must keep us to our duties. Today, Adena was slain. One of our ancient allies brought her down with a single arrow. I don't why this ally came. All I know is that this most astonishing elf kept the world from spinning out of control. We also have arrested Adena's three most trusted generals, who now will spend the rest of time in the custody of the Green Maiden. To celebrate this day, we will suspend all classes for the remainder of the week. Perhaps you might consider visiting your families. We will return to our normal routine next Monday."

A raucous cheer went up. The students quickly cleared the Scholars' Hall to make plans for the rest of the week. Sitting in the back, Affey, Michael, Minda, and Kevin were anxious to return home. Before they got a chance to go back to their rooms, the headmaster and Professor O'Riley approached them. The headmaster spoke first.

"I want to commend the four of you on your extraordinary work here. You are much more than we anticipated. You must want to go home now. Professor O'Riley will talk to you about that. I have things to attend to at the moment. I will see you all soon enough." He shook each of their hands as he left.

"Let's go to the library. It's the place where this all began." Professor O'Riley led them to the library where Master Chan Wu was waiting for them.

"Ah! The four mighty junior students," Master Chan Wu said through his laugh.

They all sat around the table as if it was the most natural thing to do.

"Are you ready to go home?" Professor O'Riley asked.

Something odd came over the four students. Now that they had the opportunity to go home, they weren't sure they wanted to.

"Michael?" asked Professor O'Riley.

"I think so. I miss my folks. But I'm not sure."

"Minda?"

"I'm not sure either. Going back to the academy may be a letdown. I know we are not qualified to stay here. I wish there was another option."

"Kevin, your thoughts?"

"Oh, I want to go home. I think this has been enough for me for now."

The three of them turned to see what Affey would say. Professor O'Riley and Master Chan Wu already knew.

Affey spoke softly to her twin sister. "Minda, this is going to be hard for you to hear. We are twin sisters. We have never been apart. I have been called to go away for a while. You cannot come with me."

Minda was starting to cry. "What are you talking about?"

Affey took her sister by the hand. "I have been chosen by the Green Maiden to be her protégé. I will be going to her this afternoon. I promise I will visit you when I can. This is my destiny and my duty." Affey didn't leave room for Minda to say more. Affey kissed her on the forehead. Affey stood up and said goodbye to Michael and Kevin. Professor O'Riley went with her. She waved goodbye as she left through the library door.

Master Chan Wu then explained what was next for the other three.

"Kevin, you may return home, or you may take a short break, say a month or so, and then you may return here if you wish. We will waive all pre-requisites for you. You may also remain back at the academy and progress as a normal student. I will need your answer by the end of the day."

"Minda, your choice is more difficult. You have displayed extraordinary gifts for mirroring. To return to the academy would be a waste of your time. Here is your choice. Return here next Monday as full-fledged senior student or withdraw entirely from the academy system and surrender all of your power. I know it's a difficult choice, but one which you must make."

Minda didn't need time to consider. "I will return on Monday. Who will explain all of this to our parents?"

"I'll get to that in a minute. Michael, your option is not unlike Minda's. We invite you to return on Monday. You too can return as a senior student, but you will be permanently assigned to Professor O'Riley. It is time we groomed a new librarian. We believe it should be you. Your other option is to withdraw entirely and surrender your powers. Your answer today as well."

Michael had a question. "Who will tell our parents?"

Master Chan Wu said, "I will. No matter your decision, you will all return home tonight. Before you arrive, your parents will have been informed. In the annals of this house, no junior students have ever been offered what you have been offered. I hope you will choose wisely. You should go and pack your things. Leave your Clonfert-House uniforms neatly folded on your beds." Master Chan Wu stood up. He gestured for his three students to go get ready for their trips home.

On their way back to their rooms, they didn't speak to one another. Each of them was sorting out what was best for them to do. They packed their things, folded their uniforms, and waited to be called. They stayed to themselves.

"Gentleman and lady," Gianni Giannotti's voice rang down the hallway, "your dear friend Gianni is here to whisk you away home." He pushed open their doors. His arms spread inviting hugs. "Oh, come now. Give us a hug. This is a special day." They all reluctantly accepted his embrace.

"Here," he said, handing each of them an envelope. "Master Chan Wu said you are to read and respond to what's inside before you can leave. I'll wait on the landing."

The three of them retreated to their rooms. The envelopes each contained the same note: *"Your decision please. Master Chan Wu."* They wrote their responses, sealed the envelopes, and returned them to Gianni.

"Well, that's that," he said. "The helicopter awaits."

The three junior students sat quietly as Clonfert House disappeared out of the helicopter windows. Minda broke the silence.

"Are you two coming back?"

"Yes," Michael said, but he didn't seem excited about it.

"Me too," said Kevin, "but I asked if I could come back on Monday. I don't need a month off. I'll miss Affey."

"We all will," Minda said quietly.

The Founding Charter for The Saint Brendan's Academies (Also Known as 'the Clonfert Compact')

(Translated from the Gaelic by
Magister Fiona O'Meara, January 1976)[2]

Preamble

We, the founding families, do on this Twenty-Second Day of February, 1414, hereby establish The Saint Brendan Academies and Clonfert House.

Purpose of these academies and Clonfert House is to train young women and men in the sciences and arts of enchantment that Saint Brendan preserved and protected at his peril. These sciences and arts are descended from those Sidha[3]. We, the founding families, wish to preserve these

---

[2] Magister O'Meara was both a product of the Saint Brendan Academy System and one of its foremost translators of the ancient Gaelic texts. All the footnotes to this document are hers.

[3] The Sidha are variously known as fairies, leprechauns, banshees, and the like. 'Sidha' is used here to include all such creatures whatever their origins. Their existence is said by some to be real.

sciences and arts which are presently threatened by forces both temporal and ethereal. Failure to establish these academies and the failure to continue to introduce enchanters into the world will result in an age of darkness and despair, something each of the founding families has sworn by blood to prevent.

<u>Guiding Principles</u>

a.   There shall be three levels of academy:

b.   Primary Academies: for those eight to eighteen years of age

c.   Secondary Academies: for those not less than eighteen no more than twenty-four years of age.

d.   Tertiary Academy (Clonfert House): for those not less than nineteen or more than twenty-seven years of age.

e.   Each academy shall be governed by the magisterium and those appointed by it.

f.   Each academy shall be a full-time residential institution where students, teachers, staff, and administration shall live in community from not

---

For others, they are more than myth and legend. Since the voyage of Saint Brendan to The Land of the Saints, the discovery of Mag Aedha *Liber Secreto*, and the success of the Saint Brendan's academies in training young women and men in the ways of the Sidha, there no longer remains any doubt of their existence.

later than 10th August through not earlier than 10th June of each year.

g. Admission to each level of academy shall be open only to those who can prove their ancestors going back not less than five generations and are possessed of some modicum of enchanter ability. Additionally, the magisterium shall establish separate, specific admission criteria, some of which are set forth below and must be included.

h. The curricula for each academy shall be set by the magisterium with the advice and consent of the Sidha Council.

i. Except for the initial assignment of faculty and staff, all successive appointments must come from the ranks of those who have received degrees from one or more of the academies, depending on the level of appointment.

j. The magisterium shall be comprised of not less than five nor more than nine graduates who have obtained degrees from all three levels of the academy. Each member shall serve a single term of nine years. Terms shall be staggered to ensure continuity of the letter and spirit of the academies.

k. Any member of the administration or staff of the academies can be removed at any time and without cause, provided eighty percent of the magisterium approves such removal.

l. The names of the academies shall forever be:

a. <u>Primary Academies</u>:
i. Saint Brendan's Academy of Enniskellin, Ireland
ii. Saint Brendan's Academy of Antrim, North America
iii. Saint Brendan's Academy of Instanbul, Turkey
iv. Saint Brendan's Academy of Delhi, India
v. Saint Brendan's Academy of Cornwall, United Kingdom
vi. Saint Brendan's Academy of Peking, China
vii. Saint Brendan's Academy of Khartoum, Africa
viii. Saint Brendan's Academy, Seoul, Korea

b. <u>Secondary Academies</u>:
i. Saint Brendan's University, Geneva, Switzerland
ii. Saint Brendan's University, Limerick, Ireland
iii. Saint Brendan's University, Kyoto, Japan
iv. Saint Brendan's University, Goa, India

c. <u>Tertiary Academy</u>: Clonfert House, Galway, Ireland

<u>General Responsibilities of Each Academy</u>
<u>Primary Academies</u>:

a. To provide foundation in the sciences and arts of enchantment

b. Character formation with an emphasis on cooperation, tolerance, compassion, kindness, and selflessness

c. Intellectual formation in logic, reasoning, persuasion, critical thinking, and listening

d. Formation of ancestral and historical understanding, appreciation, and respect

e. Development of mastery of at least four of the following skills:

f. Choice-Planting

g. Thought-Projection

h. Memory-Pause

i. Confusion-Implementation (past, present, and future)

j. Misremembrance

k. Dislocation

l. Thought-Bending

m. Erasure and Eradication

Secondary (University) Academies:
Shall provide advanced training in all of the primary skills and an introduction to Esoteric Enchantment and Transcendental Movement.[4] All students will also train in one of the oriental martial arts.

---

[4] Advances in modern science would now call 'esoteric enhancement' neuro-enchancement due to its direct application to a subject's neurotransmitters.

<u>Clonfert House, Galway</u>: training that leads to mastery of all skills from primary through Esoteric Enhancement and Transcendental Movement. Each student must master not less than two of the oriental martial arts.

<u>Admission and Length of Study</u>

<u>Primary Academies:</u>

In addition to the basic requirement stated above, admission is by invitation only from the magisterium on recommendation from its Sidha Solicitors, located throughout the world and whose purpose is to identify and recommend individuals for study.

Length of study shall be eight consecutive years. No exceptions may be granted for any reason whatsoever.

<u>Secondary (University) Academies:</u>

Admission is open only to those who have received a certificate from one of the primary academies and who are unanimously recommended by the administration, faculty, and staff of their primary academy. Length of study is thirty-six consecutive months.

<u>Clonfert House, Galway:</u>

Only those who have received their university degree with distinction, have demonstrated superior skill, are of exceptional character, and have the unanimous recommendation of the faculty of their university may be recommended to the magisterium for admission. Those who are recommended must attend a three-week retreat at Clonfert House where they will be subject to vigorous examination by the magisterium. At the conclusion of the retreat, the magisterium shall announce those who are invited to take up residence at Clonfert House to commence their studies. The final decision on admission shall rest with the magisterium. There is no prescribed length of study. The magisterium shall set the length and terms of study for each admitted student individually.

Powers of the Magisterium:

In addition to the powers set forth above, the magisterium may, as it deems fit, establish additional requirements as it deems fit. However, it may not alter, revise, or eliminate any of the requirements set forth above

Signed:

{The Founding Families}

Brian Mag Aedha	Aine Muntir Cellaigh
Finola O'Breen	Cathal Mag Flannagain
An Na Chang	Sheela O'Connail
Saatvan Anand	Niall O'Feinneadha
Colm O'Maoilduan	Jung Hua Gwan
Saohbah O'Mearedhaig	Efua Tremer
Maiwenn Aesilis	

Acceptance on Behalf of the Sidha:

Aorfie	Sindri
Urvashi	Xiezhi

Acceptance by the Foundational Magisterium

Rhianna Kelly
Giancarlo Noto
Breghit Rasmussen

Printed in the USA
CPSIA information can be obtained
at www.ICGtesting.com
LVHW011224030823
753912LV00009B/209